DON'T POKE THE BEAR!

an Emmett Love Western - Volume 2

John Locke

TELEMACHUS PRESS

This book is a work of fiction. Names, characters, places and incidents are either the product of the author's imagination or are used fictitiously. Any resemblance to actual persons, living or dead, or to actual events or locales is entirely coincidental.

DON'T POKE THE BEAR

Cover Designed by: Telemachus Press, LLC
Cover Art:
Copyright © istockphoto/16969223/mattjeacock
Copyright © istockphoto/9617262/lugo
Copyright © istockphoto/21929821/bubaone

Published by: Telemachus Press, LLC
http://www.TelemachusPress.com

Visit the author website: http://www.DonovanCreed.com

ISBN: 978-1-935670-73-5 (eBook)
ISBN: 978-1-935670-76-6 (Paperback)

Printed in the United States of America

10 9 8 7 6 5 4 3 2 1

DON'T POKE THE BEAR!

PROLOGUE

September 16, 1961

ALL THAT WAS known about Scarlett Rose Coulter, 99, is that her possessions included a bible and two wooden signs. The bible had been a present from her mother, Gentry, to mark the occasion of Scarlett's first birthday.

Scarlett had been a resident of the Caring Hearts Nursing Home six years before anyone knew she could smile, or even speak, for that matter.

When she spoke, it was only once.

An orderly bumped up against her by accident and Scarlett jabbed her hat pin two inches into his thigh.

"*What the fuck?*" he screamed.

"Don't poke the bear!" she said.

"*What?*"

Her impassive face began to twitch. Her eyes brightened. An ear to ear smile slowly worked its way across her face. The kind of smile that takes twenty years off a woman's looks in the blink of an eye. She took a deep breath, lifted her head, and yelled, "*Don't poke the bear!*"

"You a *crazy motherfucker!*" the orderly yelled. He reared back, as if to strike her, thought better about it, grabbed his thigh, and limped away at a quick pace.

Scarlett Rose watched his retreat with great amusement. She looked around the commons room, noted the shocked, ancient faces staring back at her...and started chuckling. The chuckling turned to laughter, and for the next thirty seconds she laughed harder than anyone remembered hearing a person laugh. And right in the middle of her heartiest laugh, she died.

With a smile on her face.

Fifty years have passed since that day, but people in the nursing home still talk about it. Not the ones who were there, of course, but the children who took their parents' places.

CHAPTER 1

DODGE CITY, KANSAS, 1861, is a windy, dusty-ass town. It's worse in the summer months, but even now, early April, it's a mess. It's evenin', and there's a chill in the air, so everyone in the main room of my saloon, *The Lucky Spur*, notices when the door opens.

I'm in the back of the buildin', diggin' a hole in the open area by the kitchen like I've been doin' every day for the past three weeks. It's back-breakin' work, made easier by my Chinese helper, Wing Ding. I'll tell you right off, Wing Ding ain't his actual name, but that's what someone called him years ago, and for some reason he liked it then, and likes it still. I reckon I'd shoot the first man who called me Wing Ding, and let the rest of 'em scatter. But I'll call a good man by any name he chooses.

So I'm in the hole, six feet deep, diggin' for seven.

"Got another one for you, Wing," I say.

Wing's got the hard job. He has to pull the bucket up, untie it, drop me another one, then haul the dirt forty paces away. By the time he gets back, I'll have the next bucket filled.

"He does that all day?" Burt Bagger asks.

"We take turns. Tomorrow's my day to haul."

Burt runs the local paper. For now, my jail hole seems to be the biggest news in town.

"The ground's hard from all that snow last month. Digging and hauling has got to hurt your backs."

"It does for a fact."

I don't know what sort of liniment Wing Ding uses. I only know he don't want any part a' mine. He ain't said as much, but I think it's because my witchy friend, Rose, gave it to me before headin' back to Springfield last October.

Burt watches Wing carry the bucket out the door. Then says, "Does he talk?"

"Not much," I say. "And when he does, I can't understand a word of it. But strangely, he seems to understand everythin' I say."

"Odd."

Not to me. I'm used to workin' with folks that don't talk much. My best friend Shrug is said to be a talker, but I traveled with him more'n two years and never heard him speak, though he's an uncommon good whistler.

"I understand there's talk that the town might be willing to pay you a dollar a week for the use of your jail hole," he says.

"You think?"

I finish fillin' the bucket, then put my hands behind my hips and lean back to stretch out my knotted muscles.

"I never heard of an indoor jail hole," Burt says. "My readers will want to know the benefits."

I seriously doubt the few people in town who read the *Dodge City Gazette* will care much about my indoor jail, nor the reasons for it. But when there ain't much to write about, I suppose you make do with what you've got.

For the benefit of Burt's readers I explain this'll be a good place to keep drunks till they sober up. Like most towns, Dodge has no real jail, so you'll find a couple outdoor holes here and there where people can be tossed for a night and pulled out later.

I don't care much for outdoor jail holes. Innocent people can fall in at night, and break their necks. You can cover 'em up, but if you cover 'em too tight, the men inside can suffocate. If you cover 'em in a way the prisoners can breathe, their friends can use a horse and rope to drag the cover off and set 'em free.

There's more problems.

If the hole's too shallow, them that's in it can climb out. If it's too deep, you can get seepage weeks later, and that can fill a hole in an hour's time. Of course, a big rain can drown a drunk, too. I've known drunks to drown both ways in an outdoor jail hole.

"How many will it hold at one time?" he asks.

"I can squeeze four in here, if they don't mind beatin' hell out of each other."

"Once in, looks like they'll stay put."

"They should," I say.

Before diggin' the hole, I cut a six-foot square out of my wood floor and fastened three iron hinges to it, and a rod to bolt it shut.

"The roof overhead'll keep 'em dry," he says.

"That's the plan," I say, endin' the interview.

Burt never asked, but Gentry don't like the hole bein' near the kitchen. She says the prisoners'll piss and shit in it for spite, and that'll stink up the whole kitchen and make it unsanitary. I figure to treat my prisoners well enough to discourage it. Gentry says you can't reason with a drunk, and she ought to know. She'd been whorin' five years when I met her last September, at which time she'd just turned seventeen.

I never shot a man for shittin', but reckon I would, if it upset Gentry enough.

I don't think it'll come to that, because I have plans to contain the smell. First, my prisoners'll have a bucket to do their business in. Second, when no one's in the hole, I've got a large piece of wood that'll lay flush against the openin'. And I haven't told Gentry this, but I'm plannin' to build a wall around my jail hole, after the lumber man fetches his next load from St. Joe.

The sound of many voices in the main room tells me it's time to quit diggin' and get to work. I give Wing Ding the last bucket to dump, and while he's haulin' it away, I climb out of the hole and shuck my duds right there on the kitchen floor. Then I take 'em outside, shake 'em, bring 'em back inside, and hang 'em on a peg by the door. Then I get the basin of water from the counter, take it outside, and pour it over my head and body. I hear hootin' and hollerin' from the landin' above me, turn, and see two of our whores up there smokin' pipes.

I bend over and give 'em a vertical smile, which gets 'em all worked up with laughter. Then I go back inside, slick my hair, and put on my hat and night clothes. I get about three feet into the main room when a one-eyed whore named Mary Burns comes struttin' into the main room like a Tennessee Walker with ginger up its butt. Mary sashays up to the bar, tosses back a shot of rye, puts her hands on her hips and shouts, "Who wants a free poke?"

"I do!" says Charlie Stallings.

"Then c'mere, handsome!" Mary says.

Charlie's seventeen, new to the ways of whores. He jumps up from his chair at the card table, takes a few steps, turns back for his hat, picks it up, but don't seem to know what to do with it. Finally he puts it on his head and walks up to Mary and says, "A free poke? No shit?"

Mary winds up and punches Charlie full force, right in the eye. As he spins around, reelin' from the blow, she lifts her leg and kicks his backside so hard he falls to the floor.

"Anyone else want a free poke?" she hollers.

No one else does.

About that time a young lady's voice can be heard sayin' "Well, hi there, Mary!"

All eyes turn to the steps, and every man removes his hat.

CHAPTER 2

I DRAW MY gun and race out the door. First thing I see is an old man lyin' in the street, badly wounded, and a fancy-dressed man walkin' toward him, gettin' ready to shoot him in the face from point blank range.

"Hold up!" I shout.

The fancy dressed man spins and shoots the gun right outta my hand. I dive for the dirt in the opposite direction from where the gun is flyin', and he wrongly assumes I'm outta the action. The shot he made was amazin'! A shot like I never seen or heard about. But I don't have time to admire his gunplay, 'cause he turns the gun back toward the old man's face and starts cussin' him in some foreign language. By then I've got my derringer in hand, and start bringin' it up. The fancy guy cocks his gun and shoots. But his shot goes wide, because my bullet hits the side of his head just as he pulls the trigger.

I hear people behind me comin' out of the saloon and other businesses up and down the street. I scramble to my feet and run to the old man. By the time I get to him, there's maybe ten men there, and a couple of women, includin' Gentry.

"You saved his life, Emmett!" she says.

"He ain't survived yet."

"I'll work on him."

I'm crouched over the old man, so I have to turn to look up at Gentry. "Why not the doc?"

"He's deliverin' a baby at the Manson Ranch."

"Again?" Lord, but that woman spits 'em out! "How many is that, nine?"

"Thirteen, I think."

"This'll make fourteen," someone says from the gatherin' crowd behind us.

Fourteen kids! Holy Christ! I figure Mavis Manson must fuck day and night. If only the county crops had such a fertile field to grow in, we'd never want for food. While I'm ponderin' thoughts of havin' fourteen children underfoot, someone standin' over the fancy-dressed man says, "Why this here's Bad Vlad!"

"No shit?" someone says. "How do you know?"

"I seen his show. He's the world's greatest marksman. No offense, Emmett."

"None taken," I say.

I have to admit, a guy that can shoot the gun out of my hand from forty feet, at dusk, without takin' the time to aim his weapon, well, that's a helluva shooter. I never knew anyone to be more accurate than me, till tonight. But there's no way I could've made that shot at that speed with a hand gun.

I get to my feet. "Everyone see what happened here?"

They all murmur awhile and come to the conclusion I shot the younger man to save the old one.

"Don't matter," one of 'em says. "We ain't got a sheriff anyway."

"All right, then. If two men'll carry the old guy to the *Spur*, Gentry'll tell you where to set him down. Then she and the girls'll do what they can for him till Doc comes back."

CHAPTER 3

I DON'T ENJOY killin' people. Besides all the church reasons, it's almost always messy, and you have to deal with the relatives. If there ain't no relatives, you have to deal with the corpse. In large towns that's the undertaker's job. But we don't have undertakers in Dodge, which means it's up to the dead man's family to dispose of his remains. But when there's no family present, the one who does the killin' is supposed to handle the buryin'.

I walk over to Vlad, pick up his gun, and test it in my holster. It's a nice one, better than mine, and fits nicely. I start to walk away and realize everyone else is walkin' away, too. I reckon the whole town'd be content to let Vlad lay in the street forever if it kept them from havin' to bury him. In my own case, I ain't finished the hole I been diggin' for three weeks, and have no desire to dig another one.

I know better than to ask for volunteers. I never met one yet who'd bury a stranger. First of all, there ain't that many picks and shovels in Dodge that ain't already been wore out, and second, the ground is hard as a rock.

I walk back over to Vlad, check his pockets, and find he's carryin' exactly four dollars cash. I sigh. "Anyone know if he's got a horse?"

"Jim Bigsby here?" someone calls out.

Jim runs the livery stable, but he ain't among the folks in the street.

I only know one place that'll bury a body in this part of the country, and that's Fort Dodge, five miles away. For ten dollars Major Cardigan will order his troops to bury your body for you. 'Course, you got to get it there.

"I'll pay someone to take the body to Fort Dodge," I say.

"I'll do it for four bucks," Earl Gray says, "if someone'll help me load him into the wagon."

"When?"

"I'd rather not load him tonight," he says.

"Well, we can't leave him lyin' in the street."

"Make it five dollars," Earl says, "and he can stay in my wagon bed tonight. I'll haul him to Fort Dodge in the mornin'."

There are twenty people standin' around me, but no one offers to do it for less.

I tell Earl, "For five dollars, your wife can help you load him."

"I reckon she'll want his clothes."

I reckon he's right. No scrap of paper, bit of cloth, or piece of wood goes unused in Dodge, nor any other part of

Kansas. A Dodge City wife like May Gray would be a good enough seamstress to get fifteen dollars of wear out of Vlad's clothin'. With three little ones at home, that's a bounty. So scarce is cloth for clothin' out west, when I met Gentry, she didn't own but one pair of undergarments, and hers, like many folks', was made from a used flour sack.

"May can keep the clothes," I say, handin' him the four dollars I took from Vlad. "Come see me at the *Spur* when you've got him loaded, and we'll settle up."

CHAPTER 4

IT TAKES LESS than three minutes to walk to Jim Bigsby's Livery. Jim's got a lantern lit, and he appears to be waitin' for me.

"Heard you shot the Russian," he says.

"News travels fast."

He shrugs. "Small town."

"He have a horse?"

He laughs. "Nope."

"What's so funny?"

"You'll see."

"Did he leave somethin' here?"

"Oh, yes!"

"Did he pay you?"

"Nope."

Bigsby chuckles.

"You don't seem very upset about it," I say.

"It's worth seein' the look on your face when I give it to you."

I frown. "Well, let's have a look then."

He leads me to the last stall in the barn, past nine empty stalls. Holds the lantern up so I can see what's in there.

"What the hell?"

I'm lookin' at a bear. A big, black bear.

"He's yours now," Bigsby says.

"*What?*"

"It belonged to the Russian. You killed him; that makes him your property. And you owe me two dollars for stablin' him tonight."

"What the hell am I supposed to do with a bear?"

"I was you, I'd eat it. Course, I ain't you."

I ponder that a minute, 'cause I've eaten black bear and found it tasty, unlike brown bear or grizzly, which is stringy and flavorless.

"I might be able to move some bear steak out of my kitchen," I say.

"Then pay me and take him with you."

"Now?"

"I charged the Russian four dollars a day. Two dollar minimum."

"That's crazy!"

"It's the goin' rate for bears in these parts."

I frown deeper. "You ever stabled a bear before?"

"This is my first. But at these prices, I'm hopin' to get more. Still, if I'm you, two dollars for a six hundred pound bear seems cheap to me."

It did to me too, though I felt slighted in a way I couldn't quite wrap my mind around. Then I remembered.

"It's costin' me fifteen dollars to bury the Russian."

"You could toss him in your jail hole for free, and fill it in. That'd make Miss Gentry happy, I 'spect."

We spend the next minute quiet, content to stare at the bear. I guess everyone in town must know Gentry's opinion of the indoor jail, though neither of us tells things about the other. It's our whores that seem to know everythin', and have lots of occasions to gossip with the men they serve. Now that my eyes are better adjusted to the lamp light spillin' into the stall, I get a better look at the bear's condition.

"What's wrong with him?"

"You mean his attitude, or the rope runnin' through his nose and cheek?"

"Both."

"I can't speak to his attitude, 'cause he's only been here a half hour. Maybe he's sick. The rope in his face was tied to a lead line, and that's how the Russian walked him into town."

"What about the old man? What's his story?"

"He got here ten minutes after the Russian. Said he was trackin' him and planned to kill him. Guess you kilt him first."

"The Russian winged him, and was fixin' to kill him, till I stepped in."

"And now you got a bear and a seventeen dollar debt. Minus whatever you took off the Russian's body."

"You got the lead line?" I ask.

"If you got the two dollars."

We settle up, and I lead what appears to be a very sick bear from one dusty end of Front Street all the way to First Street. We pass Vlad's body, turn right, pass two businesses, and climb the three wooden steps that lead to the porch of *The Lucky Spur.*

CHAPTER 5

NORMALLY WHEN THE front door of the *Spur* opens, the customers'll glance at who might be comin' in. This time they scream and scatter.

"What in the name of Holy Hell?" someone says.

"He's bringin' a *bear* into the house?" someone else says.

I use a loud voice to announce to the entire room, "I'm gonna tie this bear up in the far corner till I decide what to do with him. In the meantime, don't poke him."

The bear shies away from the folks in the saloon, who, seein' the timid nature of the beast, get up their courage to gather round and watch me tie him up.

"Leave him be," I say. "It's clear he's feelin' poorly, and I reckon he'll leave you alone if you grant him the same courtesy."

The second floor hallway overlooks half the main room. I look up and see three of our five whores starin' slack-jawed at the bear.

"Constance!" I holler. "Find a piece of wood and tie a string around it to fit the bear's neck."

"Why?"

"I'm gonna make a sign."

"You need some ink?"

"I do."

I see Gentry has joined the whores on the hallway. She's starin' at the bear, like everyone else in the place, not knowin' quite what to say. She gives me a quiet look that I can't cipher. But in my experience, when a man can't cipher a woman's look, it usually ain't a good thing. By the time Constance shows up with the things I need, Gentry's gone back in one of the rooms to tend to the old man.

"You want me to do the lettering?" Constance asks.

"You do write straighter than me," I say.

"What should I write?"

"Don't Poke the Bear."

She looks at me. "Who the fuck would be dumb enough to poke a bear?"

I shrug. "Rules are easier to enforce when there's a sign posted."

She shakes her head as if she thinks I'm crazy, but letters the sign anyway, and hands it to me. I approach the bear and carefully slip the sign over his head, hopin' not to get bit in the process.

CHAPTER 6

WHILE I DON'T enjoy killin' people, there's nothin' better for business.

Everyone and his brother comes into the saloon to-night, wantin' to shake my hand or slap my back. By the time the embellishin' was done, you'd a' thought I killed a dozen men, 'stead of the one. Earl Gray saunters in around ten to collect his fee.

"Where'd you get the bear?" he says.

"Won him in a poker game."

"No shit? What'd you have, two pair?"

"Nope. Just bullets."

Earl gives me a funny look, like he thinks I might be jo-shin' him. Either that or he thinks no one would bet a bear on a hand that couldn't beat two aces. But he's done talkin' about the card game. Instead, he asks, "How's the old man?"

"Not good. But I hear he's talkin' to Gentry some."

An hour ago, after puttin' the sign on the bear's neck, I tried to go up and check on the old man, but Gentry had the door locked. Lou Slips, our oldest whore, told me he'd started his death bed speech, and Gentry didn't want it interrupted.

By now the place is completely full. Them that ain't drinkin' to celebrate my shootin', are drinkin' toasts to the bear. Someone found my gun and brought it to me. I already knew it'd never shoot again, but I buy the man a drink for his thoughtfulness, and decide to keep the busted gun as a souvenir.

Every big time saloon has a piano player they call the Professor. Ours finally shows up, stumblin' in through the back entrance so drunk he walks right past the bear without givin' it a second thought. He gets about ten feet past it when he suddenly stops and turns around, as if his mind just registered what he'd seen. He jumps back and shouts, "Holy Shit!"

Everyone in the place laughs, but the Professor recovers nicely, and strolls on over to the piano, sets himself on the bench, and begins playing a bouncy tune.

Then the most amazin' thing happens: the bear jumps to his feet and starts dancin'! I mean, he steps one foot up, then the other, and twirls and puts one paw up and the other out in front, like he's holdin' a partner!

Everyone in the saloon starts hoo-rawin' and clappin', and I'm startin' to think this bear could be worth a fortune! I run over and start dancin' with him. I put out my hands and he puts out his paws, and we tap each other lightly. He still appears ill, but he's movin' around like a youngster, and just as cute, 'cept for that rope goin' through his snout and cheek.

The others realize what I've got in this bear.

"You're gonna be rich, you're gonna be rich!" they chant, while the music plays and the bear dances, and I hop around grinnin' like the village fool.

Until a shotgun blast is fired from upstairs.

The music stops, and everyone looks up to the second-floor hallway, where Gentry's standin' on the overlook, holdin' a shotgun. I can see the hole in the far wall where she shot the rock salt. While no one's hurt, I can't for the life of me figure out what's gotten into this woman I adore. Gentry points to the Professor and says, "No more music! Not another note!"

"*What?*" I say, pointin' to the bear. "Did you see him just now? He *loves* it! He's a *dancin'* bear."

Every man has his hat off, which they instinctively remove whenever Gentry makes an appearance. So exceedin' is her beauty, most men can't form a single sentence in her presence.

"Emmett," she says in a tone that makes every man go quiet, "This is your place, and I'm just your woman. But so help me, if you let the Professor play one more note, I'm walkin' out of your life forever."

I draw my gun before the first person can think to gasp, and fire six shots into the piano. Shot so fast, the Professor had no time to jump outta the way. Then I shout, "If I see or hear of any man or woman touchin' that piano again, even if you so much as brush up against it, you've breathed your last breath. Is that clear?"

I look around the room as everyone nods. Then I say, "Spread the word!"

Then I yell for Constance and tell her to draw up a sign and put it on the piano so everyone can see it when they come in the front door. I tell her the sign should say, *Music Will Get You Shot!*

I look back up at Gentry. She gives me a long look, then smiles a grim smile, and says, "Thank you, Emmett."

The way she said it was formal, but tender. Considering the anger she'd shown just before, and how sweet she were to thank me with a smile so soon after, hit me and the others like a warm fire on a frosty day. I look around the room and see tears wellin' up in the eyes of some of the ruggedest men you'll ever find on the prairie. Then, as we all watch, Gentry lowers her shotgun and turns to leave, takes a couple steps, then turns back and coos, "Could you come upstairs when it suits you, cowboy?"

The men start hoo-rawin' again, only now they're thinkin' me the luckiest man in Kansas, which calls for another round of drinks bought by this one or that. As I start headin' up the stairs, I glance back at the bear.

He's lyin' on the floor again, with the most sorrowful expression I ever seen on an animal's face.

CHAPTER 7

I DON'T KNOW all the why's and wherefore's pertainin' to women, so I can't say why Gentry seemed annoyed with me earlier, and happy with me now. I mean, I know she's happy she got what she wanted, which was to stop the music, but I don't know why she wanted it stopped in the first place. And whatever annoyed her earlier still ain't been addressed, so I got that hangin' over my head. So even though all the men below are cheerin' me on, thinkin' I'm goin' upstairs to bedpost my sweetheart, I knew when she called for me that she weren't extendin' me a romantic invitation.

This time when I try the door, it opens. Gentry's sittin' in a chair beside the bed where the old man is sleepin' peacefully. She has two lanterns goin', and I get a better look at him than I care to. He's white and pasty, and his skin is hangin so loose, he looks like a bean bag with only half the beans inside.

When I walk in, she looks up.

I start first: "You made me look bad down there, in front of them fellers."

"I know." She looks down at her hands in her lap. "I'm sorry."

I nod. "You never done that before, so I figure you must a' had a good reason."

"I did."

"That why you called me up here?"

"No. I called you up here 'cause I felt bad about how I shamed you in front of your friends. I called you up here so they'd think you're getting pussy."

"Am I?"

"No."

"Oh."

"I mean, I'm your woman. I'll give it up if that's your fancy."

"I don't want to get it that way."

"I know you don't, but that's how it'd be." She sighs, then says, "How about I explain myself, and then we can couple up after closin' time?"

I smile. "That'd make a fine name for a song."

"What would?"

"Couplin' after Closin' Time."

She shows me a curious smile, the kind she gives when I've surprised her by bein' clever or thoughtful. I can see her repeatin' it in her head. Then she says, "Why, that'd be a great song title, Emmett!"

"You think?"

"I do. Maybe you could think out a whole set of words for it."

"If only we were allowed to play music here," I say.

She smiles the exact same smile again, only this time she leaves the sweet part out. Then she scrunches her mouth and says, "Touche."

"Huh?"

"It's a French word."

I perk up. "A nasty one?"

"Monique and Scarlett used to say it. Means you got me back."

"Well, it weren't a nice thing for me to say. The second it come outta my mouth I wished it hadn't. Specially since you ain't even give me your reason yet."

Gentry nods, thoughtfully. Then says, "It's the bear."

I break out into a grin. "Did you *see* him? I mean, weren't that the most amazin' thing ever?"

"No. Sergio told me how it's done."

"Who's Sergio? How *what's* done?"

"Rudolph."

I take my hat off, run my fingers through my hair, put the hat back on. She sees me doin' this and smiles.

"What?"

"You always do that. Makes you look like a little boy."

"Wait—is that a good thing?"

"Very good thing. But I'll start over. Sergio's the dead guy." She points to the old man lyin' three feet from her. I jump back a step and reflexively draw my gun.

"He's *dead?*"

"Well, of *course* he's dead!"

She shakes her head at my stupidity, and says, "Put your gun away, crazy man."

When I do, she adds, "Seriously, Emmett. Have you ever seen a man sleep with both eyes open, makin' a dead-eyed stare?"

"I have."

"Who?"

"Turd Nelson."

She snorts. "I'm not one of your drinkin' friends, Emmett."

"What's that supposed to mean?"

"Means you're not going to get away with spinnin' a yarn about something that never happened."

I pause a minute. "How'd you know it was a yarn?"

"Think about it."

I try to think, but nothin' happens.

Then Gentry says, "The name."

"What, Turd Nelson?"

"Uh huh."

"What's wrong with it?"

"No Christian woman would name her son Turd."

"Not even Alice Crapper?"

Gentry can't help but smile, since Alice Crapper's the actual name of a Dodge City woman we met, whose name we joke about all the time. "Not even her," she says.

I look at Sergio. "How long's he been dead?"

"About ten minutes."

"Who's Rudolph?"

"The bear."

"And what's he done?"

"It's not what he's done, it's what's been done to him."
"And what's that?"

CHAPTER 8

"FIRST OF ALL, bears don't dance," Gentry says.

"Honey, I hear you sayin' that, but I seen it with my own eyes. I *danced* with him, for gosh sakes!"

"They train the bears to make it look like they're dancing. But it's horrible the way they do it."

I frown. "That bear—"

"Rudolph."

"Ru—look, can I call him Rudy?"

Gentry scrunches up her face in that cute way she does when she's considerin' somethin' important.

"Rudy's a perfect name," she says. "I like it."

"Okay then. Anyway, Rudy looked sicker than a cat eatin' persimmons, till the music started. Then he jumped to his feet and, even if he weren't dancin', he was mighty lively."

She stands and places her hand gently on my arm, and nods toward a spot that's still inside the room, but far enough that we're no longer standin' right over the dead guy.

"Emmett. The bear is *trained* to do that. He only does it to keep from being beaten."

"Gentry, no man in that room would dare put a hand to Rudy."

She sighs and speaks slow and deliberate, like she's talkin' to a child. "You and I know that, but Rudy doesn't know it." She sighs again, and this time a tear spills out of her eye.

"What's wrong?"

"You don't know what they did to Rudy, to get him to move around like that."

"Tell me."

"It hurts my heart to tell it."

Now it's my turn to sigh. "If you don't tell me what you know, I'll never understand. And I'll *never* be as understandin' about Rudy as you are."

She bites her lip and says, "They ran that rope through Rudy's nose when he was six months old. They made the hole for it by pushing a red-hot poker through his snout."

Gentry shudders. Then says, "It's the most painful part of his body, and the rope being there..." she starts to cry.

"What?"

"Every time you jerk on the rope it tears open the wound, and they jerked it open every day of his life, to keep him in constant pain. They played music, then tugged on the rope and beat him with a stick and greased his paws and forced him to stand on hot plates to make him learn how to move around like that."

I set my jaw. "Who done that to Rudy? The old man?"

"No. Sergio tries to rescue dancing bears."

"Well, he *used* to, anyway," I say.

She looks at Sergio, sorrowfully. "Yes."

And that Vlad guy owned Rudy?"

"When the circus shut down, he took the bear as payment."

I nod.

"It's worse than what I've said, Emmett."

"What do you mean?"

"When they trained poor Rudy, they broke his teeth and cut his claws and burned his paws."

I shake my head in disgust. "So every time he hears music he can't help but dance?"

"It ain't dancin', Emmett. But yes. He moves like that, and has for his whole life. He can't help it. What they did to him was pure evil cruelty."

"It ain't right, Gentry."

"No, it ain't."

We look at Sergio another minute or two. Then Gentry says, "But I'm so *proud of you!*"

"Me? Why?"

"For rescuing Rudy, and saving him from that horrible life."

This didn't seem like a smart time to tell her I planned to cut poor Rudy up into bear steak, so I say, "Well, it seemed the right thing to do."

Gentry locks her wide-set green eyes on mine and says, "And that's why I love you truly, Emmett."

"Tell me."

"'Cause you're a good-hearted man."

I make a note in my head to tell Jim Bigsby not to repeat our conversation about bear steak, since I'm pretty sure Gentry'd be against it.

CHAPTER 9

"WHAT ARE WE gonna do with him?"

"Who?" Gentry says, "Sergio?"

"No. Rudy."

"We're going to *keep* him, of course."

"Keep him?"

"Isn't that why you rescued him?"

"Uh, well, I hadn't really thought about *where* to keep him. Bigsby wants four dollars a day. We could live in a hotel for half that."

"He can live with us."

"*Here?*"

She looks perplexed. "Well, Emmett, where *else* would he live with us?"

"Bears take up a lot of space in a house," I say.

"So do jail holes."

I start to say somethin', then smile and say, "Too shay!"

Gentry smiles back and gives me a quick peck on the cheek.

"You're a fast learner," she says.

"Would a' learnt a heap more when I was a kid if *you'd* been my teacher."

"You already know lots of things I don't know," she says, frownin'. "You cipher way better than me. I'm afraid I can't teach you much."

"You can teach me French words."

"I'll see if I can remember up some more."

"If you do, I'll fast learn 'em."

Gentry nods. Then says, "About Rudy."

"Yeah?"

"We've got to get that rope out of his snout."

"That'll hurt," I say.

"Maybe doc has something to lessen the pain."

"I hope so, 'cause it's one thing to hold a man down. Quite another to brace a bear."

"Rudy'll do just fine," she says.

"How can you possibly know that?"

"I just do," she says.

And that's that.

"I should make arrangements for Sergio," I say.

"Not yet."

"Why not?"

"Your friends think we're having a poke. They'll make fun of you if you go back downstairs too soon."

"So we should stay in here with a dead man?"

"I'm willing if you are."

"Well, since they think we're doin' it anyway..."

"Oh, no you don't. I can't do it in front of a dead guy!"

"Can you at least kiss me?"

"I can do that. If it goes no further."

We kiss a minute, and get so excited we almost forget about Sergio.

Almost.

But I'm not disappointed. I'd rather kiss Gentry than poke a fine whore.

After waitin' a respectable amount of time, I leave the room and get a thunderous applause from downstairs. I turn and look back at Gentry and grin.

She winks at me.

I go downstairs and visit with the customers about twenty minutes, and then a very upset Gentry comes runnin' to the railin' and shouts, "Emmett! Oh my God! The old man just died!"

"Oh no!" I say, shakin' my head. "I'm so sorry!" I get a couple of young men to come with me upstairs to fetch Sergio in return for two dollars of bar credit. They carry him downstairs, and I go to the money drawer and take out enough for a second burial. I swear, if I have to keep buryin' people, I'll go broke in no time.

The three of us walk over to Earl Gray's house and knock on the door. When he answers, I say, "Got another passenger for your trip tomorrow."

He stares at Sergio and says, "I'll add him for another two dollars."

"You'll add him for free," I say. "It's no extra work for you, and I ain't legally responsible him."

Earl frowns.

"What's wrong?" I say.

"It don't feel right."

"It'll feel worse if I shoot you."

"Let's get him on the wagon," Earl says.

Before leavin', I give him five dollars for the burial.

"I thought Major Cardigan charged ten," Earl says.

"He'll take five to toss this one in the same hole," I say.

After the young men lift Sergio's body onto the wagon we head back toward *The Spur* and see Doc Workday ridin' in. I flag him down and ask, "How's Mavis?"

"She could birth 'em in her sleep," he says.

I lower my voice and ask, "How do you feel about working on large animals?"

He looks around and lowers his voice and says, "I agree Mavis ain't the prettiest woman in the county, but I wouldn't go so far as to—"

"Not Mavis, Doc. I'm talkin' about actual animals!"

"Oh. Well, I've been known to work on a horse or two."

"Do you have medicine strong enough to knock 'em out while you work on 'em?"

"I've used ether on horses before, but sometimes those that are helpin' me wind up passin' out."

"Is it dangerous?"

"Well, of course it is! But I ain't killed no one yet, like I have with chloroform. Ether is safer on people and livestock, but you can't light a match around it."

"Can you come by the *Spur* tomorrow mornin'?"

"Why?"

"I got a patient for you."

"A horse?"

"Yeah A big one."

"He's out back?"

"Walk on in, I'll take you to him."

"I can be there at ten."

"See you then."

CHAPTER 10

WHEN ME AND the two young men get back to the *Spur*, I'm shocked to find Gentry sittin' beside the bear, strokin' him, talkin' in his ear. I cross the floor quickly and say, "I wouldn't get that close, honey. He could kill you with one swipe of his paw."

"Rudy's a big baby," she says. "He wouldn't hurt a fly."

"My experience with bears is to assume they'll kill you first chance they get."

"Rudy's a circus bear, Emmett. He's been around people his whole life. He probably doesn't even *know* he's a bear."

I point to the empty bucket between them. "What's that?"

"It used to be table scraps. Rudy was starving!"

I'm uncomfortable with her bein' that close to Rudy, but he does seem taken by her sweet affection. I can understand that. I also understand when I'm wastin' my breath talkin' to Gentry, and this is one a' them times. So I go back to the card tables awhile and visit my gamblers. Then I go to the bar, and mix with the patrons. My main purpose here, besides ownin' the place is standin' guard. But even though Dodge City's one of the roughest towns in the west, I don't get much trouble from my regulars. And there ain't been any strangers in town lately, other than Vlad and Sergio, who are both dead.

Before closin' time, Gentry—who hasn't left Rudy's side all night—says, "It's time to take him outside to do his business."

"How do you know?"

She wrinkles her nose. "He ain't that different from you, when it comes to giving a warning sign."

I lead Rudy down the street as gently as I can, so as not to hurt his nose. When I get past the last wagon rut, we stop, and I wait for him to do his business.

He obliges.

"You're a well-trained bear," I say, then turn around and find us facing a snarlin' dog. I don't recognize the animal that's threatenin' us, and Rudy don't seem to care. There was a time I would a' shot the dog for growlin' at me and not lettin' me pass, but I've softened my tone toward killin' animals since then.

I stand aside to see what's gonna happen. I feel bad for purposely allowin' Rudy to either get bit or kill the curr, but I figure it's good information for me to have, either way. It'll show me how Rudy responds when provoked, and might possibly teach me how he fights, which could come in handy, in case he attacks me someday.

The dog jumps on Rudy, who just lets it happen. When I see Rudy refuse to fight back, I chase the dog away. Rudy ain't hurt, but would a' been, had I allowed it to continue.

Next mornin' Doc walks in the door and says, "What happened to your piano?"

"I shot it."

"Always heard you was a good shot. What was you aimin' at, a fly?"

"Nope. Just the piano."

"Well, I'd say you killed it."

He follows my look across the room and does a double-take.

"That your horse?"

"It is."

"I don't work on bears," he says.

"We're cash customers, Doc."

"Who's gonna hold it down?"

"Me, Gentry, and Wing Ding."

He looks at Rudy. "Ain't gonna be enough."

"He's a circus bear," I say.

Doc Workday walks with me to take a closer look. Since last night, I've managed to work a couple of very loose lines around Rudy's shoulders and arms that can be pulled quickly from behind to pin him down and keep him from flailin'. But poor Rudy is so used to bein' mistreated, he don't even bother to move the ropes off himself. It's pathetic, really.

"What bastard put that rope in his nose like that?"

"His trainer did that when he was six months old. It's why you're here."

"What d'you mean?"

"That's what you're goin' to remove."

"Bullshit!"

"Doc, look at him. He's so used to mistreatment we probably won't even have to hold him down."

He leans in a little closer. "That nose is infected. Probably been infected off and on his whole life."

Gentry comes up behind us. "Rudy needs you, Doc. It wouldn't be right to let him keep suffering."

Doc turns to Gentry and removes his hat. "This a dancin' bear?"

She don't bother to correct him. "He's retired."

He nods. "I won't be party to patchin' up an animal that's only gonna be abused."

"You'll get none of that here," I say, pointin' across the way to the six holes in the piano."

Doc Workday smiles. "You'd shoot a piano to keep this bear from havin' to dance?"

"I would. And if you walk in playin' a mouth harp, I'll shoot that, too."

He looks around. "Where's Wing?"

"I'll get him."

CHAPTER 11

THE OPERATION TO remove the rope turns out to be the nastiest, smelliest thing I ever been around, apart from buffalo hunters. The only worrisome moment comes when we put the ether over Rudy's nose, which he don't care for at all. His eyes go wide and I can feel a surge of power as his muscles tense. But Gentry soothes him with her talk, and he quiets back down right quick. In the end, it's just like Gentry predicted, and Rudy comes through it just fine.

While Rudy rests up from his surgery, Wing Ding and I make him a body harness from some old horse reigns. I know I won't be able to hold him back if he's determined to go forward against my will, but Rudy don't seem like the kind of bear that's gonna be trouble. I guess the proof'll be in the puddin'. After finishin' the harness, Wing and I go back to diggin' the indoor jail hole. It's my turn to haul the dirt to the toss area, and as the day turns to afternoon, I dump another load and look up to see Earl Gray drivin' his wagon toward town faster than need be. I look behind him to see if Indians are attackin', but there's no one chasin' him that I can see.

So fast is his approach, I drop the empty dirt bucket and circle around the buildin' to see if he plans to stop in front of my place. When he does, I run up to him.

"We're at war!" he shouts.

"What? Who's at war?"

"The whole blamed country!"

"What're you talkin' about?"

"They just finished takin' your money for the burial when a telegraph message come through. The North has declared war on the South!"

"Wait a minute. Which side are we on?"

"Damned if I know! But we better figure it out soon!"

"Maybe we should hold a meetin'," I say.

"Maybe we should."

"We can do 'er in my place."

Word gets around and a couple hours later there's about forty people in the *Spur's* main room. I start by sayin', "As you probably all heard by now, Earl was at Fort Dodge this mornin', and learned the North declared war on the South. In January we became a Union free state, so I assume we're with the North. At the same time, we're a western state, with no militia. I'm not countin' the soldiers at Fort Dodge, since there ain't enough of 'em to help either side, right Earl?"

"I saw eight or nine," Earl says, "plus a couple officers and a cook. There might've been one or two more, but I doubt it."

"The Fort Dodge soldiers are there to protect settlers from Indians," I say, "so I doubt they'll be reassigned to fight southerners. But if anyone's got any information about any of this, we'd love to hear it."

There's a lot of mumblin' and grumblin', but no one gets overly worked up, since none of us are quite sure which side we're on, or even if the war involves us. After ten minutes of brave talk and idle threats directed at nameless people who may or may not be fightin' against us, we shut down the meetin', and everyone gets drunk.

CHAPTER 12

THE NEXT MORNIN' Gentry and I take Rudy for a stroll. Most of the town folk know about Rudy, and only the local dogs ain't happy to see him. Gentry is pretty as a picture, all decked out in the new dress she bought with the money we stole from Roy Ellsworth, back in Grand Junction. Ellsworth was a scoundrel who was marryin' mail order women and stealin' their money. He apparently killed a couple of 'em, too. That don't justify stealin' his money, but Gentry and me did it, anyway. Afterward, we spent a few days in St. Joe, where we had a little vacation, and Gentry built her wardrobe. Then we traveled west, to purchase *The Lucky Spur* from a friend of mine who'd been wantin' to retire.

Gentry's been a respectable woman ever since, though she runs a string of whores out of my saloon and card emporium. We ain't tryin' to hide the fact she used to be a whore, since two of the whores she knew in Rolla are workin' for her. The other one she knew from Rolla is One-Eyed Mary Burns, who runs her own whore house out of *The Third Street Saloon.*

We walk Rudy a mile out of town to a place we've picnicked before. Gentry wanted to bring Rudy here because it's an area where tubers are known to be plentiful. She wants to show Rudy a good time, but also wants to see if he has the instincts he'd need to survive without our help.

The weather's warmer than it's been, but the sky's gray, and there's still a faint chill in the air. Not enough to let us see our breath, but enough to make us glad we're wearin' jackets. Spring's tryin' to poke through, but it's a week or two away yet.

We stop in the dip of a wide valley.

We're nervous about lettin' Rudy run wild. Got no idea what might happen. After lookin' around to make sure the three of us are completely alone, we hold our breaths, let go of his leash, and wait to see what happens.

And nothin' does.

After standin' there a minute, Rudy plops down at our feet.

Gentry and I look at each other and bust out laughin'.

We're determined to show him how to dig tubers, so Gentry and I try to make him get up. She pulls on his body harness and I push from behind, but he just rolls onto his back and yawns. Gentry motions for me to follow her, so I do, and we leave Rudy where he is. About a minute later he realizes we've walked off, and he makes a frightened bleatin' sound and gets to his feet. When he spies us near one of the few trees in the area, he waddles over to us and lies down at our feet again. I shrug, and start kickin' at the dirt beneath the tree, till I uncover a tuber. I'd a' thought the smell would be enough to get Rudy up and diggin', but he's content to lie there.

I reach down and dig it out with my hands and lay it on the ground an inch from Rudy's nose. He sniffs it, but gives it no further attention. I look at Gentry. She shrugs. Then she slaps my butt and starts runnin' away. I chase her a few yards, catch her, and turn to see Rudy watchin' us. I tag Gentry, and she starts chasin' me. She tags me and I chase her. The whole time we're taggin' and chasin' and laughin', Rudy watches from a distance, with no change in his expression.

Finally we're wore out, so we give each other a hug, and walk back over to Rudy. I bend over to pick up his leash and he taps me on the back, hard enough to make me fall. I holler, "What the—" but when I turn toward him, Rudy jumps to his feet and runs about ten yards, and waits.

Gentry's face is full of life. She claps her hands and says, "Go tag him, Emmett!"

So I run toward him, and tag him, and start runnin'. It takes him about two seconds flat to catch me and swat me to the ground again. I roll head over heels two or three times before comin' to a stop.

"Tag him again, Emmett!" Gentry yells.

"He's likely to *kill* me!" I shout back.

"Don't be a sissy!" she yells. "He wants to play!"

"Why don't *you* tag him, then?"

"I would, but he wants to play with his daddy."

"His what?"

She laughs.

I make another run toward Rudy, and he lets me tag him. This time he tries to swat me before I can get away. But I see it comin', and duck under his paw. He gets a funny expression on his face and makes that bleatin' sound, and I take off runnin'. This time when he comes thrashin' toward me, I dive onto the ground, and he trips over my legs and rolls over. I look up and see him do somethin' I never seen an animal do before.

Gentry sees it too.

"Oh, my God!" she says, her voice full of wonder. "He's laughing!"

He *is* laughin'.

I never seen anythin' like it! This goofy bear is rollin' around on his back, laughin'.

On the way back home, Gentry's quiet.

"You're workin' somethin' out in your mind," I say.

"I am."

"Tell me."

"I'm thinking about Rudy laughing."

"It was somethin' to hear, all right!"

We walk a few minutes without speakin'. After awhile Gentry says, "Rudy hated to dance, but I don't think most people knew that."

"I'd guess that's right."

"He made people happy when he danced."

"He did."

"They were laughing at the *Spur*, night before last."

"When Rudy danced? They were laughin' like crazy!" I agree.

"He probably heard people laugh his whole life."

"Probably did."

"You think he knew he was making people happy?"

"Probably."

"You suppose he's been around people so long he's picked up our traits? Like laughing?"

"I can't think of a better explanation," I say.

CHAPTER 13

A WEEK PASSES, with no news about the war. Wing Ding and I finally finish buildin' the jail hole, and now I'm almost hopin' someone acts up tonight, so I can try it out. About eight p.m., a man comes by the saloon and says he's recruitin' men under thirty years of age who know how to shoot.

"There's a rumor President Lincoln is going to be kidnapped and killed," he says. "I'm working with Senator James H. Lane to recruit some Kansas patriots to move into the White House and protect the President from his enemies."

"How long would we have to be there?" one man asks.

"No more than a month," he says.

"What's it pay?"

"Pay? You'd accept pay to protect the President?"

"I would," he says.

"I would, too," another man says.

"I'm keen to help," a third young man says, "but I'm needed at home, unless there be pay."

The recruiter sighs and gives up and heads for the next saloon. I can't for the life of me figure out why the President can't find some young men closer than Kansas to protect him from his enemies.

A couple hours later, a young man gets up from a card table after losin' his money, takes two steps, and faints. I rush over to him and splash some water in his face, and ask, "When's the last time you ate somethin'?"

"Two days ago."

I recognize him as the young man who said he was needed at home if he couldn't be paid to guard the President. I help him back to the kitchen, where Emma Nickel's doin' the cookin' tonight. We don't have a regular cook, so the whores take turns. None of 'em are any good, but Emma's the worst. Still, some food is better than none, and since this young customer has lost all his money, I tell Emma to fill him up.

The young man is about three inches shy of six feet, maybe twenty-two years of age, with a handlebar mustache that makes his baby face look silly. But Emma likes what she sees, and begins puttin' a flirt on him that renders her virtually useless as far as keepin' up with the food orders goes. For his part, the young man appears to find Emma distasteful, and tries his best to ignore her advances.

The first thing you notice about Emma is when she speaks, she fondles her breasts without realizin' it. While that makes her quite popular among the whore house customers, it's distractin' to the card players. Also, she's got six fingers on one hand, four on the other. Emma whored in Rolla, Missouri, at Lick and Casey's Dance Hall, down the street from where Gentry used to whore. She made the trip with us to Dodge a few months back. When I bought the *Spur* and decided to run whores, we offered Emma a spot, for old time's sake. She's enthusiastic in bed, regardless of who the customer might be, which is as good a quality as any whore can have. But when I hear her offerin' this hungry man an apple bob, I decide to come to his rescue.

"Emma, you're fallin' way behind on the supper orders," I say.

"I need help, Emmett. It's too busy tonight."

I call Hester down to help.

"No fair! I cooked for six hours last night!" she whines.

"Sounds like you need a cook," the kid says.

"Don't suppose you want the job?"

"Nope. But thanks."

"What's your name, son?"

He starts to speak, pauses, then says, "William Clarke."

The way he paused before answerin' makes me wonder if he's still feelin' fainty.

"If you don't mind my sayin', you ought not to be a card player."

"Why's that?"

"When the others saw they could bluff you, they clipped you good."

"Bluffin's dishonest."

I laugh, then say, "Well, like I say, cards ain't likely to be your livelihood. What else are you good at?"

"Gambling's in my blood, but I'm a school teacher by trade."

"Well hell, we need a school teacher right here, if you're willin' to give up the gamblin'."

Emma puts a plate of beans in front of Bill Clarke and asks if she can feel his muscle. He sighs and flexes his arm. She giggles and grabs his crotch, sayin', "That ain't the muscle I was referrin' to!"

"*Jesus*!" he says.

"Emma?" I say.

"Yes, sir?"

"Cook."

"Where's Hester?" she says, rubbin' her nipples.

Bill's eyes grow wide watchin' her do it.

"Hester's on her way. Now quit fondlin' your tits! And that goes for our school teacher, as well!"

She frowns. "Everyone else has a beau. Don't see why I can't have one."

Bill shudders.

"Sorry 'bout that," I say. Then add, "We *do* need a school teacher. Right now all we have's a buildin', and a woman who's got the learnin', but not the time to devote. I s'pect the town could afford to pay a decent wage if you offer your services full-time."

Bill digs into his beans and don't stop to answer till he's worked his way through half the plate.

"Thanks for the offer, but I can't."

"Why not?"

Between bites he says, "I taught school in Illinois, then headed west, joined the army, fought in the Utah War.

When that ended, I tried the gamblin'. Was always better at dice than cards, but couldn't make a livin'. Too many cheats. Two years ago I moved to Lawrence and taught school. But I'm done with that now, 'cause of the war."

"What's the war got to do with not teachin' school?"

"I aim to join the Missouri State Guard."

"Lawrence is east of here. As is Missouri."

"I traveled to Pearl, to see if my Aunt and Uncle could spare some money to fix me up with a horse and guns. They done what they could, but it weren't enough. I hoped to win enough at cards to complete my provisionin'.

"Well, I won't arm a man to shoot other Americans, but I can fill your belly and give you a place to spend the night."

"I'm obliged," he says.

"When you're done eatin', we can use a dish cleaner. When that's done, you can take the second room on the left, upstairs. You'll find it clean, and no one will bother you. Tomorrow mornin', if you're willin' to sweep, we'll feed you again, before you head out."

He nods. "That'll be fine. Again, I'm much obliged."

The next mornin' Gentry and I take Rudy outside of town, west this time, figurin' if he ever runs off he'll be able to find his way back, if he's familiar with the area. Not that we think he'll get far if he *does* run away. Due to the abuse his feet have suffered, he's limited as to how far he can travel. After we get where we're goin', we start playin' tag and continue playin' until all Gentry and I have to do is shout, "*Rudy: tag!*" and he tries to swat me. If he misses and I start runnin', he bounds after me. And every time he tags me, he me, he knocks me ass over heels and laughs his silly head off.

We stop to rest awhile, and I notice Gentry's beamin' like a proud mama. I ask, "What's got you so pleased?"

"Rudy knows his name!"

"You sure?"

"Positive. Let go of the harness and stand with him, and I'll prove it."

I let go of the harness and rest my hand gently on Rudy's shoulder. Gentry walks twenty paces and shouts, "Come here, Rudy!"

Rudy's ears perk up.

She repeats the command, fillin' her voice with enthusiasm.

Rudy yawns and lies down on the ground.

Gentry walks back over to us and says, "Well, disregarding that, he still knows his name."

"Maybe he thinks 'come here' means take a nap."

Gentry pushes me and yells "Tag!"

Rudy jumps to his feet and puts his arms up and grins. He's waitin' for me to tag him so he can knock me down again.

"How come he never plays tag with you?" I ask.

"He doesn't want to hurt me."

Before I can say, "What about me?" she says, "He knows you can take it."

I look at Rudy and think, *If I came upon him at dusk, on the trail, he'd scare the shit outta me!* But here, in this environment, knowin' him as I do, I can't imagine him raisin' a paw to strike neither man nor beast.

Next thing I know, he's runnin' away from us, almost as fast as my horse, Major, can gallop!

"What the heck?" Gentry says. "Rudy!" she hollers. "Come back here this *instant*!"

But Rudy doesn't so much as slow down. Gentry takes a deep breath, ready to shout at him again, but I motion her to hush. When she does, I close my eyes and listen.

I don't hear a thing except Rudy thrashin' off in the distance, gettin' further and further away from us. Then I open my eyes and say, "Uh oh."

"What?"

"Honey bees!"

"So?"

"Where there's bees, there's honey."

"So?"

"There ain't nothin' in the world a black bear loves more than honey."

CHAPTER 14

BY THE TIME we get there, and by "there" I mean a hundred feet away—Rudy's covered in honey and bee larvae, and cryin' from bein' stung by the swarm of bees around his face.

"Why doesn't he run away?" Gentry says.

"Once a bear gets started on a hive, he won't quit no matter how bad he gets stung. He'll eat the live bees, the larvae, the honey, the honey comb—he can't help himself."

I look at Gentry and see she's really concerned.

"He'll be okay," I say. "His fur's thick enough to protect him from most of it. His eyes and nose'll swell, and he'll be sore and cranky tonight. But believe me, he's as happy as a kid with a new toy."

"He can't stop?"

"It's sort of like how he has to make them dancin' movements when music is played. Only this time nature's makin' him do it, 'stead a' men."

"But he gets something out of it," Gentry says.

"He does. Accordin' to Rose, honey has all kinds of medicine in it. It'll help Rudy get stronger, and probably help him fight against getting' his nose infected from the operation."

"If the bees don't hurt him worse."

"He'll be okay."

By the time Rudy's done eatin', he's a sticky, nasty mess. We want to lead him to the river, but he's havin' none of it. He lies down to take a nap. No matter how hard we try to coax him, there's nothin' left to do but sit there all afternoon with him, till he's finally ready to get some water. By then it's dusk, and the river's too far in the opposite direction.

"I don't know how you're going to get him clean tonight," Gentry says, "but he can't come in the house like this."

"Me?"

"You're the one who knows all about bears and honey."

I sigh.

An hour later, me and Wing Ding decide the best way to clean Rudy is to rub dirt all over him, then take a wet cloth and try to scrub the honey and dirt out at the same time. Of course, the bee stings have him all swollen up, and he's cranky.

It takes us two hours and requires three separate inspections from Gentry before she'll let him back inside, but

Wing is happy for the work, since it's income he weren't expectin'. I find Wing so agreeable and helpful I decide to offer him a full-time job on the spot. As I stumble around with my words, tryin' to explain what I'm offerin', he startles me by saying, "I happy work for you. One dollar day. Start eight. Stop eight. One hour lunch. No windows. Okay?"

I stare at him.

"All this time you could speak English?"

He shrugs.

I frown. "What do you mean, no windows?"

He says, "I kidding about windows. Start tomorrow?"

I nod, still bewildered about his ability to speak.

"One more thing," he says. "Food terrible. I cook lunch and supper for all."

"I agree our whores ain't suited to cookery," I say. "I'll be glad to give you a shot at it."

CHAPTER 15

RUDY'S IN NO condition to go for a walk the next mornin', but Gentry and I've grown accustomed to the time together and decide we don't need Rudy as an excuse. Wing Ding saddles our horses and packs a breakfast that smells so good I want to dig in before we leave. But I hold off after thinkin' how much fun it'll be to picnic on a blanket in a field with Gentry.

The Arkansas River runs just north of Dodge, which is why there are so many trees. It's also hilly, compared to the land east of Dodge. It's a clear day, not a cloud in the sky, and while the temperature is cooler than warm, I'm comfortable with my jacket off. Like most women I know, Gentry is cold-natured, and keeps her coat buttoned up tight. She's wearing a burgundy hat today, and for some reason the breeze is so slight, she doesn't have to pin it to her hair. That's rare for Dodge, which is consistently windy. We choose a spot a quarter mile below the highest hill, where the grass is tall and green. The river's a hundred yards west of us.

I tie the horses to a low tree branch, and Gentry spreads a blanket on the ground and sits. I take a minute to admire her silhouette. Gentry's always been slim and well-built, but when I met her last September, her face was littered with pimples somethin' awful. Worst case of pimples I ever seen. My witchy friend, Rose, slathered some type of smelly yellow poultice on her face every day for several days. When Gentry come out from under all that yellow stink, she had the prettiest complexion I ever seen. Rose used to travel with me from Springfield, where she lives, to Dodge City. For two years me, Shrug and Rose ran a business where we brought whores and mail order brides west from Rolla and Springfield, Missouri, to Dodge by horse and wagons 'cause the railroad and stage coaches don't service eastern Kansas. Of course, it won't be long before that changes, since progress is headin' our way from both ends of the country.

Gentry's posture is perfectly straight. She looks like she's posin' for a portrait, sittin' on the picnic blanket in front of me. I can't imagine holding a pose like that for any length of time without hurtin' my back, but she's young and flexible and learnin' how to be cultured, and could probably sit that way for hours if she had to. It's my plan to relieve her of that pose and get her on her back, where I can hug up against her before we take the time to enjoy the breakfast Wing made for us.

I'm thinkin' these thoughts about Gentry as I remove our lunch from my saddlebag. What I'm holdin' is some sort of sandwiches wrapped in a cloth. I hold the bundle to my nose and take a whiff and wonder if it could possibly taste as good as it smells. I smile at Gentry and say, "I think hirin' Wing Ding might turn out to be a good plan."

She says, "I'm happy about it. I've grown quite fond of Wing. He's dependable, industrious, and very respectful of me and the ladies."

"And from the smell of this breakfast, he's a fine cook as well," I place the bundle next to her on the blanket.

She starts to say somethin', but suddenly our attention is drawn to the other side of the hill where a shot has been fired.

"Sit tight!" I say, as I turn toward my horse.

"I'll do nothing of the sort!" Gentry says, jumping to her feet.

"It's probably nothing. I'll just ride over and take a quick look."

"We'll do it together."

"Fine."

I turn back, grab the food, and put it back in my saddle bag. By then, Gentry's got her left foot in the stirrup. Her horse is shyin' slightly, so I wait to make sure she swings her leg up and over without fallin' off. She does. I get on my horse quickly, and we gallop up the hill. Twenty feet before crestin' it, we climb off our horses and tie 'em to a large, dead tree branch on the ground. Then we creep toward the crest.

I hear 'em before I see 'em: three cowboys yellin' and laughin'.

Gentry hears 'em, too, and says, "I don't like the sound of this."

"They're drunk for sure."

I motion her to lay on her stomach, and I do the same. Then we crawl to the topmost point of the hill and push some grass out of the way and look.

We both see it at the same time.

"*Oh my God!*" Gentry says. "It's Shrug!"

It *is* Shrug, my former scout and best friend. The cowboys have shot him and are in the process of strippin' him naked. One has placed a rope around his neck and tightened it.

"Whatever the hell this thing is," one of 'em shouts, "I'm gonna sell it to the Chinese in Dodge!"

"It's some sorta man, but he looks like a grasshopper!" another one yells.

It's true Shrug is seriously deformed. He was trampled in a stampede as a child and lucky to survive. As he healed, he grew more sideways than tall. So badly formed is Shrug, he can't ride a horse. And yet he's the fastest, most dangerous man I ever met. He can kill in pitch darkness with a single throw of a rock. There's no better rock chucker in the world than Shrug, and no way these yahoos could've got the drop on him without resortin' to trickery. I look at the trampled grass nearby, and the wound in Shrug's back, and can guess what happened.

These bastards probably saw him comin' from the top of the hill, where you can see for a couple of miles. One of 'em probably laid down in the grass where it's been trampled. He probably cried out for help. Shrug come along to help, leans over the man, and gets back-shot by someone hidin' in the tall grass. The third hombre probably had the horses on the east hill and rode down just before Gentry and I got here. I look around to make sure there aren't more of 'em lurkin' about.

Gentry says, "We've got to *do* something, Emmett. He'll bleed to death!"

"I'll take care of this," I say. "But you need to clear out."

"What are you *talking* about? I'm his friend, too! He *needs* us. I can help bandage his wound."

"Gentry, look at me."

She does. She knows from my tone I'm serious.

"Shrug's an uncommon proud man. If he thinks you've seen him stripped naked, helpless like this, he'll never want to be around you again."

"But Emmett–"

"He's my best friend, Gentry, besides Rose."

"I thought I was your best friend."

"You're the woman I love. They're my friends. Of course you're my friend. But it's different."

"Shrug is *my* friend, too."

"I mean it. Go back and get the blanket and pretend none a' this happened. Don't speak a word about it. If anyone asks why you're back without me, tell 'em we had a quarrel and you came back on your own."

"A *quarrel?*"

"Please, Gentry. He's my only friend, besides you and Rose. I need you all in my life, and this could ruin it."

"That's ridiculous."

"I'm done talkin' about it. I aim to kill these bastards and save my friend. But I won't do it till you leave."

She sighs. She's angry, but knows I'm serious. "Fine. But come straight to the *Spur* so I can take care of him."

"I'll try, but he probably won't let me bring him into town. You know how he is about bein' seen by people."

"Please try."

"I will."

"Emmett?"

"Yeah?"

"Can you kill these men?"

"I can."

"Are you certain?"

"Yes."

"Promise me you won't get killed in the process."

"I promise."

She takes one more look. They had him naked and were tryin' to get him to his feet. Probably plan to parade him through Dodge naked, with the rope around his neck.

"Poor Shrug," she says.

"He'll be okay. But you gotta get movin'."

She turns to leave, then turns back and says, "I don't understand you men, and your prideful ways. I find it hard to believe you'd let him die before you'd let me help."

"Believe it."

"Emmett?"

"Yeah?"

"Whichever one shot him..."

"What about it?"

"Make him suffer."

"If you'll get movin' I aim to make 'em all suffer."

"Okay. When will I see you again?"

"I have no idea. But don't worry."

"Right."

She finally leaves. I give her a couple minutes to fetch her blanket from the picnic area, then I walk over to my horse and remove my rifle from the scabbard.

CHAPTER 16

THE FIRST TWO are easy.

I start with the guy on the horse, who's got the rope tied to his saddle horn. I fire a quick shot that hits the side of his head, then quickly squeeze off a second round that catches another guy in the neck. Unfortunately, the sound of the first shot has caught the ear of the third guy, who suddenly realizes his two friends have been shot. The first guy's dead, the second moans loudly while bleedin' out. But before I can shoot the third one, he lies down and pulls Shrug on top of him. He works his gun out of his holster and puts it to Shrug's head. He's lookin' in my direction, knows the shots came from this general area because of the smoke from my rifle barrel, but can't see me.

I keep my rifle trained on him and wait a few minutes and realize we're at a standstill. I slide back down and walk to my horse and remove the bundle from my saddlebag, open it, and eat one of the sandwiches. It's unbelievably good! So good that if anyone but Shrug was down there, I'd eat the other one, too. I open the canteen and drink a few swallows, then resume my position on the hill and wait for an opening. After ten minutes, I notice the man's left foot has moved about a foot away from Shrug's body.

I squeeze off a shot and hear him cry out in pain. He slides his gun down his body, props it against Shrug's hip, and shoots a couple of poorly-aimed shots in my direction. But I'm out of range for a handgun. Even Bad Vlad couldn't hit me from there.

I stand to my full height and wave my arms and call him names, tryin' to get him to shoot at me to use up his bullets. But he realizes what I'm up to, and resumes puttin' the gun against Shrug's head.

"I'll kill him, so help me!" the man yells.

"Do it, then," I holler back. "What do I care?"

"You care," he yells, "or you wouldn't a' got involved."

"I'm not involved. I just like killin' cowboys and sellin' their horses and guns."

Shrug knows my voice. I can't tell if he's unconscious or not, but he's not movin'. If he's conscious, he'll wait till the time is right, and then make his move. When he does, I'll get a clear shot.

"Where are you men from?" I holler.

"None a' your business!"

I go back to my horse and get my canteen and sit on the side of the hill in plain sight. The man under Shrug's body can't stand the fact I'm sittin' right out in the open like that, sippin' from my canteen. He takes careful aim and squeezes off a shot that lands ten feet shy of my feet. I'm surprised how close he got, but know he won't try again, since he's down to three bullets. We both know he can't reload, because if he tries, he'll lose his grip on Shrug, and if Shrug moves as much as a foot away, I'll kill the guy.

He yells, "Your friend is bleedin' to death."

"He ain't my friend. Shoot him if you like."

"You don't mean that."

"Try me."

I'm not worried about Shrug bleedin' to death. He's been livin' with Rose at least part of the last few months, and Rose always makes us drink a birch bark tea that heals us faster and keeps our wounds from gettin' infected. If Shrug had been gut shot, or hit in the center of the back, I'd be on this bastard like a hog on sassafras. But I can tell Shrug's wound ain't a mortal one.

The guy's friend stops moanin'.

"You killed my friends," he yells.

"Don't fret. You'll be with 'em soon."

"Turn around and leave, and I'll spare your weird-lookin' friend's life."

"He ain't my friend. What I'll do is have your horses."

"Why don't you come get them?" he yells.

"I will," I say. "In time."

I *do* wonder why the horses haven't scattered. They're the best trained animals I ever saw. All three of 'em still standin' there, though none are tethered. Just seein' horses behave like that makes me want to cuss Major.

An hour passes. Then I holler, "How's your foot?"

"Fuck you!"

Another hour passes, and the foot that's been shot slides out from under Shrug again. I squeeze off another shot and laugh when he screams in pain.

"You think that's funny?" he yells.

"I can see where it might not be as funny to you."

A few minutes pass and he yells, "All right. You can have our horses."

"Thanks."

"If you promise to let me go, I'll send them on up."

"How're you gonna do that?"

"I'll tell them."

"How dumb do you think I am?"

"Teddy!" he yells. "Go up the hill!"

Suddenly, one of the horses turns and looks at me. Then trots up the hill and stops a few feet in front of me. Rose might a' got a horse to do that, but she's a witch. I work with my horse Major every damn day and have for years, but if I don't tie him to somethin' stout, I'm on foot.

"Send the others on up."

"Do I have your word you'll let me go?"

"Yes."

"I don't believe you."

"I get that a lot."

"Teddy!" he yells.

Teddy trots on down the hill and stops a few feet away from him. I really hate the bastard for what he's done to Shrug, but I got to admire his ability with horses.

Then he shoots Teddy and yells, "I got two more bullets. I'll shoot both the horses. Then you'll get nothin'."

I can't abide a man that'll shoot a horse. Not to mention my best friend. If ever I came across a man that needed killin', this were him.

I try to keep the anger out of my voice when I yell, "You kill those horses and there's nothin' to keep me from killin' you. Plus I get the saddles and guns, and while they ain't the same as horses, that's more'n I started with this mornin'."

I stand up and take careful aim.

"What're you doin'?" he shouts.

The guy's tall, and Shrug's wide, and so far it's been workin' to his advantage, except that he can't completely hide beneath Shrug without exposin' some part of himself. I walk a few yards to the right, to get a different angle, and see him tryin' to maneuver Shrug's body in such a way as to cover himself better. From this vantage point, I see his ear is exposed. That ain't worth a lot, but it's somethin', and will serve to discourage him some more.

I take the shot and hear him yell.

Then it dawns on me that if Shrug was gonna make a move, this'd be the time to do it.

But he doesn't.

Which gives me great concern.

I mean, I'm lookin' at him, and can see that he's only shot through the shoulder. It ain't a bad wound. But Shrug hasn't moved so much as a muscle all this time. I start wonderin' if maybe when he got trampled as a kid, his insides got moved around as well. What if his heart or some other vital organ is in a different place than most people's? What if he's dead? Could he actually be dyin' while I'm fartin' around with this guy?

As if he can read my mind, Shrug whistles the sound a wood warbler makes.

"Shut up!" the guy beneath him yells, and hits the side of Shrug's head with the butt of his gun.

I start chucklin', realizin' what's goin' on.

Shrug is layin' there, on top of this guy, butt naked, enjoyin' the fact I'm whittlin' him down, one shot at a time! He could make his move and let me end it with a single shot, any time he wants.

But he's havin' too much fun.

Which is why I love Shrug!

A few minutes later, Shrug moves his head a couple of inches, and I shoot half the guy's nose off!

"You *bastard!*" he yells.

A few minutes goes by and he shouts, "I think you're out of bullets."

"You're right," I yell. "Climb on out."

Shrug allows his right foot to fall off the guy's leg, exposin' his ankle. I shoot it and he screams in pain.

"Where the fuck you learn to shoot like that?" he yells.

"My uncle was a gunsmith," I say. "Used to build rifles by hand. Let me test 'em. I been shootin' rifles my whole life."

"I seen better!" he yells.

"Maybe," I holler. "But riflin' is all about practice. I figure to get a lot more today, shootin' holes in you."

"I ain't givin' up!" he shouts. "You can shoot me all day, but I ain't goin' nowhere!"

"Good!" I holler. "'Cause I ain't never had this much fun killin' a cowboy!"

CHAPTER 17

I WALK A few more yards to the right, and watch the guy below try to move Shrug to compensate for the angle. His right foot has been shot twice, and he can't feel it when Shrug lets his leg fall to the side. When he does, I shoot the guy in the foot for the third time.

I give him credit for trainin' horses and bein' one tough bastard, but this third shot in the foot makes him start to cry.

"Let me go!" He yells. "I ain't done nothin' to you!"

He's been shot three times in the right foot, once in the left ankle. I've shot one of his ears off, and half his nose. All these wounds are bleedin', but he still manages to keep Shrug on him in such a way that it's hard to get a clean shot without hittin' my best friend.

Shrug knows this, so every now and then he moves a different part of his body. Since I don't know which part he's movin', I can't find the openings quick enough most of the time. But when Shrug suddenly lifts his right arm, I put a bullet in the center of the guy's left hand.

"*Damn!*" he yells, and I can imagine Shrug smilin'.

An hour goes by, durin' which time I shoot the rest of his nose off, and put two more slugs into his left hand.

Then I walk back to my horse.

"You leavin'?" he yells.

"Yup. You outlasted me!"

A few minutes later I come back and sit where I'd sat earlier.

"I knew you weren't leavin'!" he shouts.

"Glad to see me, are you?"

"You didn't shit that quick," he yells. "You must a' taken a piss."

"Nope. I was out of bullets. Had to reload."

"You're wastin' a lot of ammunition on one man!" he shouts.

"Can't help it! You're a tough man to kill."

"Damn right I am!"

I wait a few minutes, watchin' him suffer. Then I say, "I feel like I ought to tell you somethin'."

"Fuck you!"

A few minutes pass. Then he says, "What were you gonna tell me?"

"The guy that's layin' on top a' you."

"What about him?"

"He can kill you anytime he wants."

"Oh yeah? So why don't he?"

"He's havin' too much fun."

I take careful aim with my rifle, and wait for my words to sink in. Suddenly the guy lifts his gun up to smash it into Shrug's skull...

...Leavin' me enough room to shoot the gun out of his hand, just like Bad Vlad taught me.

I walk down the hill, noticin' he still hasn't moved out from under Shrug. Probably can't. When I'm standing next to 'em I say, "How'd you train your horses to do that?"

"I ain't tellin' you nothin'," he says.

"Pity. Those are damn fine horses."

"They'll stomp you to death first chance they get."

I frown.

"Shrug?" I say. "Kill him."

And Shrug does.

CHAPTER 18

I HELP SHRUG get his pants on and lay him on his side so the wound is facin' up. I can tell while helpin' him that the bullet is still in his shoulder. We got to get it out before he can start healin', and hope he don't lose too much blood in the process.

I carefully get his shirt back on, then take mine off, fold it as small as I can, and place it inside his shirt over the wound. Then I arrange him so he's layin' on his back, against the side of the hill with his head higher than his feet, which allows the hillside to keep pressure on his wound.

"I bought that saloon we talked about last fall," I say.

He nods. Then lifts his right hand and rubs his thumb and fingers together while raisin' his eyebrows.

"We do all right. But it ain't as profitable as I was led to believe.

He moves his hand to his face and makes a sort of mask, then slides it down. That's his sign for Gentry.

"Yep, we're still together, and she's still the prettiest woman in Kansas, as far as I'm concerned, and a great business woman too. Why, if it weren't for Gentry's whores, we'd be losin' money. I think that'll change, now that I got all the repairs behind us. Oh, and I built an indoor jail hole. First one ever."

Shrug looks at me curiously, holds his thumb and index finger over his nose.

"Yeah, Gentry says the same thing. But I got plans to solve that."

He gives me a skeptical look.

"Reason I mentioned the saloon, I got Gentry and five whores there who can take care of you, and a clean bed you can sleep in. You know three of 'em. Emma, Leah, and Hester."

He nods.

"There's a doctor in town who can dig this bullet out of you usin' ether that's so strong so you won't even feel it. At least till the next day, when it'll hurt like hell."

Shrug smiles, but shakes his head.

I sigh. "Figured you'd say that."

Then I say, "Will you be okay here while I fetch my horse?"

He nods.

"Okay then, I'll get Major. I've got a sandwich for you, too. Finest one I ever ate. Where's your water?"

He motions to his right.

"I'll get it."

I start walkin' in the direction he pointed, to the tall grass, and in minutes I find the leather straps that lead to the canteens he started his trip with. I also notice the two remainin' horses are still standin' where they were hours ago, when the shootin' started. I 'spect the horse he shot belonged to one of his partners, since a man would shoot his own horse last and the worst one first.

While I don't approve of mistreatin' animals, it crosses my mind for the second time that if Teddy was the worst of their horses, mine deserves a good cussin'. I won't cuss Major, 'cause ornery as he is, we been through a lot together. Havin' said that, I might give these other two horses a try and see if they'll follow my direction.

Then I realize I don't know their names.

Probably so well-trained they won't do anythin' for me less I call 'em by their names.

Shrug can't use his left arm without feelin' severe pain, but his right hand is all he needs to enjoy Wing Ding's sandwich.

"Helluva sandwich, right?"

Shrug nods. Then raises his eyebrows.

"Don't know what's in it. Some sort of Chinese cookin'. Guy named Wing Ding. He's the one helped me dig my jail hole. I hired him last night to work full-time. He's gonna take over all the cookin' duties. You can eat like this every day if you come to my place to heal."

He smiles.

Then I get an idea.

"Look. I know you don't like towns, and don't like bein' seen. But I can wait here with you till it's dark. Bring you in the back way. No one'll see you."

He ponders it.

"Did I mention I've got five whores who live on the same floor?"

His lips curl into what I've come to recognize as a smile.

Then, to my surprise, he nods.

"You will? You'll let me take you to town?"

He nods again.

"Well, that's wonderful! Gentry'll be thrilled!"

Then Shrug makes a fist, and opens it and wiggles his fingers. That's his sign for Rose.

I frown. "You never said why you left Rose. I thought you'd be happy there."

He moves his hand, makin' signs until I realize what he's tryin' to say.

"Are you tellin' me Rose is on her way here?"

He nods.

"Why?"

He points at me.

"She's comin' to see *me*?"

He nods again.

"Why? I mean, that's wonderful, but why? Is there somethin' wrong?"

He nods.

"What?"

He shrugs.

It's difficult gettin' detailed information out of Shrug. What makes it worse is, apparently he can speak perfect English. At least, accordin' to Phoebe, who traveled with us the last time Shrug scouted for me. So I don't know it to be true, but accordin' to Phoebe—who never lied that I know of—Shrug not only speaks perfect English, but French too, and has a beautiful singin' voice to boot.

But he won't speak to me. I don't know why. Guess maybe I offended him those first two years we traveled together when I assumed he couldn't speak, and never bothered to ask if he could.

"You were what, a day ahead of her?"

He shakes his head and holds up four fingers. Then holds up three more.

"Seven hours?"

He nods.

I do the math in my head and say, "So Rose should be comin' through here in what, about three hours?"

He holds up four fingers and points behind us, and makes a curvin' motion, then moves his hand straight up, which I understand as bein' his sign for a mountain.

"You mean this big hill here?"

He shakes his head, no.

"Well that don't make sense," I say, knowin' he can hear the frustration in my voice. "There ain't no mountains around here. Wait—are you talkin' about the cliffs of the Arkansas River? Past the sulfur pits?"

He shakes his head again.

"Good, 'cause that makes no sense, either. Rose'd follow the trail through Newton like we always do. Then, ten miles north of Dodge, she'd head due south, which'd put her about a half mile east of here, just like always."

He signs it again, slowly.

I frown and say it out loud as he signs it. "When Rose comes here...she'll travel around the...*mountain?*"

He makes a sign for horses.

"What? No oxen?"

Shrug shakes his head, then holds up three fingers, twice.

"You're tellin' me Rose is travelin' with six horses and no oxen? Why, that's insane!"

He shrugs and starts signin' it again, from the start.

I repeat, "Rose is drivin' six horses, no oxen, and they're goin' to circle some fargin' mountain that ain't even around here."

Shrug starts quietly laughin' till the tears come out of his eyes, and I wonder if maybe the pain from his wound has affected his mind.

I say it again, changin' up the words a bit, tryin' to make sense of it.

Then it hits me.

"You shithead!" I say.

Then I start laughin', toss my head back and sing, "She'll be comin' round the mountain when she comes!"

CHAPTER 19

FOR THE NEXT couple of hours we sit and I talk while waitin' for Rose to show up. I don't bother workin' on Shrug's wound, knowin' Rose is a better doctor than any I've met. In all the time I've known her, she's only lost one patient, and that one had been gored repeatedly by a hydrophobic bull. By the time it's late afternoon, I get around to sayin', "Oh, and we got a bear livin' with us!"

Shrug shows me his quizzical look.

I say, "Yup, right in the house, in the corner of the main room."

He cocks his head and I say, "Black bear. Maybe 600 pounds."

I start tellin' him how Bad Vlad shot the gun out of my hand in near pitch dark, and how I wound up with Rudy after tryin' to scrounge up burial money. I got sidetracked and told him about how we're at war, only we don't know much about it. Then I get back on the subject of Rudy, and how he danced that night, and how Gentry threatened to leave me, and how I shot six holes in the piano. Halfway through that part of the story, and before I got to the part where the Doc operated on him and how we take him for walks and play tag and such—Shrug touches my arm, signalin' me to hush. We both listen. I have wonderful eyesight, and a fine pair of ears. But I don't hear or see anythin'.

Shrug makes a fist, opens it up, and wiggles his fingers.

"Rose is here? Already?"

He nods.

"Okay. I'll go find her and we'll bring the wagon to you."

Turns out I don't need to go huntin' for Rose. As I crest the hill I see her headin' straight for us. I ride on up, and we wave as I approach.

"How bad is he?" she says.

I wasn't surprised Rose knew about Shrug bein' shot. She always knows these sorts of things without bein' told. Because of that, and because she's a great doctor and cook, and can talk to animals and serpents, and because she's a great traveler, and a woman of wealth, and able to read other people's thoughts and put her own thoughts in people's heads, and because she can disappear from view right before your eyes, and jump fifteen feet straight up in the air onto tree limbs—Rose is a helluva handy woman to have around.

When she ain't scarin' the shit outta you by doin' all them things.

"He'll be fine," I say, "Now that you're here. How are you, Rose?"

She smiles. "Life is good. Let's get Wayne in the wagon, and we can catch up on everything while I work on him."

I notice she's taken to callin' Shrug "Wayne." Phoebe used to do that. On the trip from Rolla to Dodge last September, our mail order bride, Phoebe Thayer, took a shine to Shrug early on, which was a good thing for both of 'em.

"How's Hannah?" I ask, as we round the hill toward the spot where Shrug's waitin' for us. Hannah's the little orphan girl we met on our last journey. Like Rudy, she'd been abused throughout her young life, and Rose took pity on her and took her back to Springfield to raise.

"Hannah's blossoming. Roberto and his wife are watching her for me, so she'll probably speak fluent Spanish by the time I get back."

Roberto is Rose's ranch hand, and has been, ever since I met her.

"Shrug gave me the impression you came all this way because of me."

"I did."

"Why's that?"

"Someone's coming for you, and I need to be here."

"Who's comin'?"

"Bose Rennick."

CHAPTER 20

ROSE AND I lift Shrug into the back of her wagon and place him on his side so she can work on his wound. It's still light enough for her to check his shoulder. She hands me back my shirt, and I pour some canteen water on it and wring out what blood I can, before puttin' it back on. Rose tears Shrug's shirt away from the wound, looks back at me and frowns.

"Bullet's still in there," she says.

I nod.

She sighs and reaches for her doctorin' bag. I've been on the receivin' end of her work more times than I care to remember, but this is the first time I remember Shrug needin' medical attention.

She scolds him with an angry tone. "How did this happen?"

Without waitin' for a response, she gives him somethin' to drink. I recognize it as a potion that takes the pain away, though I don't know what it's called. I do know it takes several minutes to work.

"You were careless, weren't you," she says to him. It came out more like a statement than a question.

Rose says, "We've talked about this before. You've got to stop trusting people. They don't like our kind."

That throws me for a loop.

"What kind is that?" I say.

She looks at me. "We're different. Surely you know that."

"Well, I know you been accused of bein' a witch, but Shrug ain't never been, to my knowledge."

"He has special powers."

"Like what?"

She narrows her eyes. "Are you truly this dense?"

"Probably."

"The man survived being trampled by a stampede as a child. He can hear things more than a mile away. He can see almost as far as I can. He senses things I, myself, sometimes miss. He can see in the dark. He's fleet of foot to rival a horse for short distances, and can best any animal over bad terrain over long distance. He can kill a bird in mid flight with a rock—"

"And he don't sleep," I say.

"Exactly. Didn't a thing like that ever raise your curiosity?"

"At first."

"And later on?"

"Later on I just thought of 'em as bein' things Shrug was good at."

"Like talents?"

"Uh huh."

"Can you do any of those things?"

"Well, I'm talented at some things."

"You're better at some things than anyone I know. But can you do things no one else can do?"

"I thought I could shoot better than anyone till I met Bad Vlad."

Rose sighs. "Will you just accept the fact that Wayne is different?"

"Okay."

We're quiet a minute, while she gives Shrug another drink from the bottle that takes pain away. Then I say, "How many different people are there in the world?"

I hear Shrug laugh at my question.

"We're *all* different, you chucklehead!" Rose says.

"I mean, how many are different in the ways you and Shrug are different?"

"None."

"None?"

"None I've ever met." She leans over and puts her head at the same angle as Shrug, so they're face to face. "Have you ever met anyone like you or me before?"

He shakes his head.

Rose says, "There's just the two of us."

I ponder her comment so hard she has to touch my arm before I realize she's asked me somethin'.

"Sorry, I didn't hear you."

Rose smiles. "That's alright. I know what you were thinking."

"Tell me."

"You were wondering how it's possible that the only two people in the world with special powers happen to be your two best friends."

"Well, it *does* seem a hell of a coincidence."

I stop ponderin' a minute to look at their faces, to see if I can read some special meanin' in 'em, but all I can see is they're both smilin' a strange smile.

CHAPTER 21

WHILE ROSE CUTS the bullet out of Shrug's shoulder, I think about Bose Rennick, the outlaw she claims is after me. If she's right, I've got problems.

The first time I ever laid eyes on Bose Rennick, I was ridin' through Jacksboro, Texas, and he was chained to a tree, with three lawmen guardin' him. Later I heard he got away. Next time I saw him was on the trip west, when I met Gentry. Bose and his partner, Sam Hartman, got the drop on us, and would a' killed us 'cept for Rose spookin' their horses. The three things you want to know about Bose Rennick is he's a stone-cold killer with more than twenty notches on his gun, he's got enormous, crazy eyes, and he has the richest, most beautiful speakin' voice a man could possibly have.

As evil a man as Bose Rennick is, Sam Hartman is worse. He's widely considered the cruelest man who ever lived. In the western frontier of 1861, that's sayin' a lot.

While Rose always turns out to be right about her premonitions, they don't always happen at the time she expects 'em to. That ain't necessarily her fault, as she explains, because things like weather and sickness and accidents and coincidences can come along to delay or speed up events. The best value about this premonition regardin' Bose Rennick is I can be on my guard. 'Cause whether he comes tonight, next week, or next month, the important thing is to be ready for him. And if Sam Hartman is with him, as I s'pect he'll be, that's a tall order to deal with if a man ain't prepared. And even if he is!

"Are Bose and Sam travelin' together?" I ask.

"I don't know."

"Any idea when Bose will show up?"

"Sometime after you become sheriff."

I give her a close look. "You sure about that part?"

"Positive."

"Good," I say, much relieved. "Since I have no plans to be sheriff, I guess I got nothin' to worry about."

After Rose sews Shrug up with her catgut, we wait a couple hours till it gets dark enough to sneak Shrug into town without lettin' him be seen by too many. We tie the two outlaw horses to the back of Rose's wagon and I ride Major into town with Rose followin' close behind. When we get to the back of the *Spur*, Rose and Shrug stay in the wagon, in the shadows. I tie Major to the rail post, and wave to the whores smokin' on the balcony.

"Heard you and Gentry had a big fight!" Leah says.

"You need a place to sleep tonight, you can cuddle up with me," Constance says.

I tell 'em to go back inside and call for Gentry. They do, and seconds later, my Gentry comes tearin' down the steps and throws herself in my arms and hugs me like a child hugs a puppy. When she hears a sound behind me, she jumps back.

"Rose?" she says.

"Hi Gentry!"

Gentry and Rose exchange a hug, and Rose drags her over by the lamp light to get a better look at her face.

"Your skin is absolutely flawless!" Rose says.

"Thanks to you!" Gentry gushes.

When Gentry turns her attention back to me, I say, "You won't *believe* who else is here!"

"Who?"

"Shrug."

"*What*? Where is he?"

Rose laughs. "You don't have to pretend, Gentry. Wayne knows you were there."

"But–"

"It's okay. He's embarrassed, but he loves you both. If you don't talk about it, he won't either."

"How did he find out?" I ask.

"He heard you and Gentry talking on the hill this morning."

"He told you that?"

"He did."

"When?"

"When we were following you to town."

"You've heard him speak?" Gentry asks..

"Of course!" Rose says. "He speaks to everyone except Emmett."

"Why is that, do you suppose?" Gentry asks.

"You'll have to ask Wayne."

CHAPTER 22

SHRUG IS STRONG as an ox, able to climb the back steps without my help, though I fuss with him all the way up to the landin', tryin' to get him to take my arm in his. Truth be told, he gets up the stairs quicker and easier than I do, which is a sad thing to have to admit.

Gentry puts Shrug in the first room and helps him get situated. I head back down the stairs to help Rose carry some of her belongin's. We put her in the second room, so she can be next door to Shrug, and doctor him as necessary. Rose has no trouble enterin' the room through the back door, but by the time she takes three steps, she freezes.

A terrible look comes over her face, and she starts to swoon.

"Rose! Are you okay?" I rush over to her, but she waves me off. She starts to stagger, and reaches for the bedpost at the foot of the bed to steady herself. But as she touches it, she gasps and withdraws her hand as if she'd been burned by fire.

"What on earth?" I say.

She's pale as a ghost. She reaches her hand out to mine. I take it.

"Get me back outside," she says.

"But–"

"Please!" she whispers.

I pull her out the back door and close it. We stand on the landin', where the air is cool enough to see our breath. I decide not to ask how she is, figurin' if she wants me to know, she'll tell me. I've got a good hold on her arm, in case she starts to faint. While I don't want to intrude with my words, I do want to know if she's still feelin' lightheaded, so I cock my head to the side to get a good look at her face, which is hard to see, 'cause the outdoor lamp light is below us, and the bedroom lamp is dimmed by the curtains. I can't see her expression, but I hear her breathin' gettin' more regular.

"Is it the room?" I say, knowin' it can't be the room.

"Yes."

"What about it?"

"I can't be in there."

"Well, you can stay in our room. Me and Gentry can bunk in there, if that suits you."

She turns and puts her hand on my cheek. "You don't understand. I can't be in there, but I *have* to be."

She's right. I don't understand. "Why would you stay somewhere you don't want to be? You don't have to stay in that room. We can switch, or if you'd rather, I'm sure Shrug'll be happy to trade with you."

"I have to figure out what he's going to do."

"Who, Bose Rennick?"

"The man who was in this room," she said, in a voice so low she seemed to be mumblin' to herself. "Do you know him?"

I think a minute. Then say, "I do."

She sits down on the edge of the landin', with her feet on the steps. Puts her hands on either side of her head, coverin' her ears, and looks up at the sky.

"He's not here," she says.

I'm confused as hell. Not knowin' what else to say, I ask, "Is that a good thing? Or a bad one."

When she turns toward me, her face is somehow easy to see. Rose has always been pale complected, her face more likely than most to pick up whatever light is available. But right now it seems to be glowing.

"If he were here, you could kill him."

"Kill him? He's just a kid."

"Tell me everything you remember about him."

"Well, his name is Bill somethin'."

"*Think*, Emmett!"

"Bill Clarke. Calls himself William. He's a school teacher. Fought in the Utah War, whatever that was. Tried his hand at gamblin. Been teachin' in Lawrence, Kansas the past two years. Said he went to Pearl to ask his Aunt and Uncle for money, 'cause he wanted to get outfitted to soldier with the Missouri Guard. The Missouri *State* Guard."

We were quiet a minute. Then I said, "Why would you want me to kill him?"

"He's going to do something horrific."

"He is?"

She nods.

"When?"

"I don't know."

Gentry comes out and says, "What's wrong?"

Before I can say anythin', Rose says, "I felt faint just now, after climbing the steps. It reminded me I haven't eaten since this morning. Emmett was kind enough to keep me from falling."

"Well, I can take over," Gentry says. "We can go downstairs and eat. Emmett, you can join us after."

"After what?"

"Your meeting."

"What meetin'?"

"The Mayor wants to talk to you."

"The who?"

She laughs. "The Mayor."

"Since when do we have a Mayor?"

"I don't know. The way he said it, sounded like everyone should know."

"Well, who is it?"

"I don't know. He's a small man with a giant, beautiful voice."

"Like Bose Rennick?"

"Exactly. Except that no one has a voice quite like Bose Rennick."

I knew that to be true. "And he's short?"

She smiles. "Unless there's a better word for it."

"When does he want to meet?"

"Right now. He's downstairs, waiting for you. Along with the rest of the Town Council. And wait till you see *them!*"

"The what?"

Gentry sighed. "Let's don't go through all this again. Go downstairs, meet the silly men, shoo them along, then meet Rose and me in the kitchen."

I look at Rose. "Will you be all right?"

"Yes. Gentry can help me unpack, and we'll get a bite downstairs."

"You're going to love our new cook!" Gentry says.

"I'm sure I will."

As Gentry leans to pick up one of Rose's carpetbags, Rose and I exchange a look that tells me she's determined to spend the night in the room she don't want to be in.

CHAPTER 23

"WHO'RE YOU FELLERS?" I say, shakin' hands.

We're sittin' at the most secluded card table in the main room, which is still pretty noisy.

"I'm James Ha-a-a-averhouse," the tiny guy says.

I figured him to be a stutterer. "Haverhouse?" I say.

"No. Ha-a-a-averhouse. Mayor Ha-a-a-averhouse."

I stare at him, wonderin' if he's bein' smart with me. I look him over and decide his name's the biggest part of him. The two men with him are opposites. One's the tallest, thinnest man I ever seen. The other is the widest. Now that I think on it, Mayor Ha-a-a-averhouse is the shortest man I ever seen. With a giant, speech-givin' sort of voice that puts me in mind of Bose Rennick's, though like Gentry said, no one's got a voice like Bose. The Mayor's voice might coax a woodchuck from its hole, but Bose's voice would make it march right into a fryin' pan.

"When did you move to Dodge?" I say.

"Long time ago," the Mayor says. "Can't remember, it's been so long."

"Uh huh."

I'm sittin' with a full-grown man who's less than three foot tall in a town of less than 150 people, where I live and work. I believe I'd a' run into Mayor Ha-a-a-averhouse if he'd been livin' here even twenty minutes.

"You have a businesses here?"

"Of course." He looks at the other two, and chuckles. They chuckle back. Of the four of us, I'm the only one who seems confused.

"You're tellin' me you own a business here in Dodge City."

"Yes, of course! How could I be Mayor if I didn't own a business or live in Dodge?"

"That's what I was wonderin'," I say.

"I own the feed store."

"Which feed store?"

"Only one feed store in town I know of," he says.

"G. Reed's Feed & Seed?" I say. "The one that's two doors from this very saloon?"

"None other."

"You bought it from George Reed?"

"I did."

"When?"

"I'd have to look it up to tell you the exact date. Seems like years ago. But that can't be right, can it?"

"No, it can't."

Mayor Ha-a-a-averhouse says, "I can't believe you haven't seen me around town all these months."

"Seems unlikely, don't it?" I say.

The Mayor points to the other two fellers. He says, "I can understand how you might not recognize me, since I tend to blend into the crowd. But surely you know these men."

"Can't say I do."

"You're jokin'."

"Do I look like I'm jokin'?"

"No. Please allow me to do the honors."

"Go ahead."

"Mr. Emmett Love?"

"Yeah?"

"It's my pleasure—nay, sir, my honor!—to introduce you to my dear friends and fellow council members, Bob, Robert, and Harry."

I look at them.

"There ain't but two fellers here."

"Yes, of course."

"You named three men."

"When?"

"Just now."

The tall guy holds out his hand. "I'm Bob Robert," he says. "This here's Harry."

I nod. "How long you boys been in town?"

They look at each other. Bob Robert says, "What's it been Harry?"

Harry says, "Gosh, I dunno. Long time, hasn't it?"

Bob Robert looks back at me, "A long time."

I scoot my chair back a foot, in case I need to go for my gun.

"What's this town council do?"

"*Do?*" Bob says, lookin' at Harry.

Harry says, "We represent the views of the town in response to various public consultations."

I stare at him a long time before speakin'. "You fellers have business with me?"

"We do," the Mayor says.

"Speak it, then."

Harry clears his voice, gettin' ready to speak. I put up my hand and say, "Not you. Someone else tell me."

The Mayor juts his tiny chin toward the far side of the room. "Your bear," he says.

"What about him?"

"He's in violation of the town's safety laws."

"What safety laws?"

"He poses a constant danger to the town."

"Who says?"

They all look at each other. Mayor Ha-a-a-averhouse says, "Why, *we* do! We've held meetings, debated the situation, accepted arguments both pro and con, and come to the decision your bear has to go."

"For the safety and well-being of the town," Bob Robert adds.

"What other safety hazards are on your list?"

They look at each other again. Harry starts to speak. Again I hold up a hand. "Not you." I look at the Mayor. "You."

"Well, so far that's the only item on the list."

"Uh huh. And who enforces these laws?"

"Well, we were sort of hoping *you* would."

"Me?"

Bob says, "We'd like to offer you the position of Sheriff."

"Sheriff."

"That's right."

"You want me to be Sheriff, so I can force myself to get rid of my own bear."

"It'd make things a whole lot easier," Harry says.

I start to get up, but change my mind.

"Who appoints the Sheriff?"

"We do."

"How much would I get paid?"

"Half of whatever you collect in fines."

"Fines for what?"

"Breakin' the law."

"Who makes the laws?"

Mayor Ha-a-a-averhouse smiles. "We do."

"You know what I think?" I say.

"What's that?"

"I think you're part of the circus that disbanded."

"Circus? Why—because of the way we're dressed?"

I take a minute to look at the way they're dressed. Their clothes are the only thing normal about 'em. But then I decide it don't really matter if they're circus folk or not. Dodge City needs a Mayor and Town Council, and a Sheriff, too. I'm just not sure I want to be part of it.

"Only way I'd agree to be Sheriff is if I get to make the laws," I say.

"I could live with that," the Mayor says.

"Me too," Bob Robert says. "Harry?"

"Me too," Harry says.

"Who gets the other half of the fine money?"

"We do," the Mayor says.

"So if I say the bear stays?"

"You'd have to declare it a law."

"How do I do that?"

"You write it on a piece of paper and we vote on it. Then we put a special seal on the paper, sign, and record it."

"And if you vote against it?"

"That wouldn't be in our best interest."

"You mean the town's best interest."

"Yes, of course."

"How about it," Mayor Ha-a-a-averhouse says. "You want to keep your bear?"

"I do."

"Produce the document," he says to Harry.

Harry removes an official-looking document from a leather case I never saw till now, and places it on the table. It reads:

> *"By special order of Sheriff Emmett Love, as approved by Mayor Ha-a-a-averhouse, and Town Councilmen Bob Robert, and Harry, there shall be no bears allowed in Dodge City from this day forward, with the sole exception of the circus bear known as Rudy, who currently resides at The Lucky Spur."*

I look the document over and frown. “You ain’t got a last name?” I ask Harry.

“It’s Haverhouse,” he says.

I look at the Mayor, who explains, “Harry just uses his first name because his last name is difficult to pronounce.”

“Uh huh. So you two are related?”

“We share the same mother, but different fathers.”

“A’ course you do.”

The Mayor says, “Before you sign it, we need to swear you in.”

They do, then Harry pulls a piece of cloth out of his pocket. It has five points, and contains the word *Sheriff*, which appears to have been printed by a child.

“What’s that?”

“Your badge, of course.”

“Want me to pin it on?” Bob Robert says.

CHAPTER 24

WHEN I ENTER the kitchen, Wing Ding's gone, Hester's scrapin' dishes, and Gentry and Rose are sittin' at the small table where she and I take our meals. Rose appears to be feelin' much better. I've noticed over time that Gentry has that affect on nearly everyone. It dawns on me that the two prettiest women I've ever seen in my life are in the same room with me, and both have special, though different, feelin's about me.

"What did the strange men want?" Gentry says.

"To make us get rid of Rudy."

"*What?*"

"Simmer down. I fixed it where they can't bother him."

"How?"

I pull the piece of cloth from my pocket.

Gentry's face lights up. "You're the *Sheriff*? Oh, Emmett, I'm so *proud* of you!"

"Proud?"

"Uh huh."

"Why's that?"

"You can kill people without getting arrested."

"Well, that's a plus."

Rose looks at the cloth badge and says, "Bose Rennick will be here soon."

"You know when, exactly?"

"No. But soon."

"And Sam Hartman?"

Rose shrugs. "No idea."

"Have you met Rudy?"

"I have."

"Did you speak to him?"

"Of course."

"Well?"

"Well, what?"

"What do you think about him?"

Rose smiles. "He's noble."

"Noble?"

"Yes."

"What's that mean, in relation to a bear?"

"Means he has an outstanding moral character, and carries himself with quiet dignity."

"He's really bright, ain't he!"

She don't say anythin' and looks a little uncomfortable.

"Well, ain't he bright?"

"No."

"What?"

"I'm sorry, Emmett, but he's dumber than baked beans. Dumbest animal I've ever met."

"What?"

"But he's noble."

"He seems so bright."

"To you, maybe."

I look at Gentry. "You gonna say anythin'?"

She shrugs. "I thought he was smart too, but I don't speak bear."

To Rose I say, "Are you mad at me for some reason?"

"Mad? No. Why do you ask?"

"It ain't polite to insult Rudy's intelligence. He's been through a lot. And you may be a good friend, but I don't approve of you disparagin' what I know to be a helluva smart bear. Maybe you don't speak black bear as good as you think you do. You probably spoke grizzly to him by mistake. Of *course* he wouldn't respond to grizzly."

Rose and Gentry look at each other and bust out laughin'.

"What's so funny?"

Gentry says, "I put her up to it."

"Which part?"

"I told her to say Rudy was dumb."

"Why would you do a thing like that?"

"I wanted to see if you'd defend your son."

"He ain't my son. He's a dang bear."

"Well, you defended him like a son."

Rose winks at me, mouths the words, "*Sorry Emmett.*"

"You ought to be ashamed of yourself," I say, though she knows I don't mean it.

Gentry walks over and kisses my cheek. “You know what I think?”

“No,” I say, pretendin’ to pout.

She kisses me again. On the lips, this time. Then says, “I think *you’re* noble, too.”

CHAPTER 25

THE WHORES SLEEP two to a room, and each night a different one can either sleep alone or have an overnight guest. That takes care of three of the bedrooms. Shrug has the first guest room, Rose the second. Gentry and I sleep in the last bedroom, at the end of the hall. There's a hallway door to our room, then the bedroom door. I built the outer door so I could hear anyone tryin' to get to us from inside the buildin'. But like the other rooms, our back door leads to the balcony. Our early warnin' system from the back is the steps themselves. They creak somethin' awful, and I don't fix 'em on purpose. You won't get past the third one without wakin' everyone in the house.

We have three rules after closin' time. First, I have to know whoever's stayin' in the overnight whore's bed. Second, no one comes in after closin' time. Third, no one goes outside after closin' time. The outhouse is only twenty steps from the back of the buildin', but bad men often lurk in the shadows near the outhouses women and girls are known to use. Gentry knows a dozen town women who've been violated on their way to or from their privies in the middle of the night. Some of 'em know who done it to 'em, but most won't complain, for fear their husbands, sons, or brothers could get killed tryin' to defend their honor. Now that I'm sheriff, I s'pect I'll hear these complaints privately. I'd love to learn who these men are, and kill 'em.

It's embarrassin' even to our whores, to have to do their business in the middle of the room, in a pot or bucket, when someone else is sittin' or sleepin' a few feet away. But over time you get used to it. The worst part is when one gets an upset stomach, 'cause everyone else in the house is gonna know it. If someone's in a really bad way, I'll get my rifle and stand guard while they go to the outhouse. But that's a last resort, because the likelihood of bein' ambushed while standin' up there on the balcony is high.

Up there, in the relative dark, I'm a sittin' duck.

So tonight, knowin' Bose Rennick and probably Sam Hartman are headin' our way, I'm extra careful to tell everyone my back is up, and not to do anythin' that might make me start shootin'.

Somewhere in the middle of the night, I hear a noise outside on the balcony, despite all I've said. I look out the window and see Rose sittin' on the steps. I open my back door and call her over with a quiet whisper.

"Sorry, Emmett," she whispers. "I can't be in there any longer."

"Did you see your vision?"

"I saw enough."

"You need your sleep, and I do, too. You can bunk with Gentry. I'll take your bed tonight."

"You don't feel the evil in there?"

"Rose, I've spent weeks in jail cells that have been slept in by the evilest men who ever drawed a breath. I guarantee you, no twenty-two-year-old school teacher ever lived that can rob me of a good night's sleep. Plus, I've slept in that room several times, when Gentry's been mad at me."

She chuckles, softly. "Gentry would be angry if she heard you tell that."

"Well, good thing she's asleep then," I whisper.

"You sure you don't mind?" Rose says.

"Of course not. Sleep tight. And be sure to lock the back door when I leave."

She does, and I enter the room she fears, feel my way around in the dark for the bed, climb in, and sleep like a baby.

CHAPTER 26

THE QUALITY OF our window glass ain't great, and there ain't an abundance of birds in town. But every now and then the sun will hit one of our bedroom windows in such a way as to cast a reflection. When I hear a thump like the one that wakes me up this bright, crisp April mornin', I know the barn swallows are back.

I don't like barn swallows. They fly into Dodge in early to mid April and leave in September. So far I've owned the *Spur* durin' the off season, but I heard that these birds'll drive horses, dogs, cats and people crazy all spring and summer long.

The one that woke me up is lucky I didn't spin around and shoot it when it hit my window. But even while soundly sleepin', I know to listen for the steps creakin' before I think to shoot. Now that I'm awake I hear some voices downstairs, and smell somethin' wonderful I ain't smelled in months.

Rose's cookin'.

I hope Gentry's down there learnin' some of Rose's kitchen secrets.

I climb down the back stairs, taking Vlad's handgun with me to the outhouse. When I'm finished with my mornin' ritual, I come to the back, wash up at the pump we share with the dry goods store, the feed store that's under new ownership, and Mrs. Dunphy's Boardin' House. Surprisingly, no one's out back this mornin', so I take time to shave by the small, broken mirror someone tacked to a small tree by the trough. When I'm done, I walk back upstairs, lock the back door, and go out the front and down the hall. As I look over the railin', I see somethin' that don't make sense.

There's six people sittin' at different card tables, as if savin' 'em for games, but we ain't even open for cards yet.

By the time I hit the bottom step, eveyone's raisin' their hand to get my attention. I stop where I am and say, "What's goin' on?"

Everyone starts talkin' at once.

I calm them down and learn they've all been told I'm Sheriff, and they've got problems for me to solve.

I notice Gentry across the way. She can see by the look on my face that I'm frustrated. They all want to talk, but none want to talk where the others can hear. So I give 'em each a number, and tell 'em to wait at the far end of the room, and I'll talk to each of 'em in the quiet corner.

"You expect us to stand by the bear?" one lady says.

I recognize her as Mrs. Plenty, the very prim and proper wife of Leah's best customer. Leah's thin as a rail and has a scar that runs from the far corner of her eye to the side of her nose. The scar is at least twenty years old. She earned it at the age of ten, in a knife fight with another young whore. By all accounts it had been a bloody battle, and by the time it was over, Leah took the other girl's life. But the wound on Leah's face had been stitched so poorly, her earnin's were never what they should a' been. She traveled with us to Dodge last September, and I managed to get her a spot with a Madam friend of mine, Mama Priss. But even Priss couldn't afford to keep her, so Gentry took pity on Leah, and gave her a place upstairs, where she's managed to attract a couple of regular customers, includin' Mrs. Plenty's husband, Peter. Whatever Leah's doin' for Pete, it's workin', 'cause if Leah's not available, he waits. Still, she don't get much traffic. If it weren't for Gentry and the buffalo hunters, she'd be whorin' in a hog ranch.

"The bear won't hurt you," I call out, loud enough for her to hear.

Mrs. Plenty looks nervous. "I've never been in a saloon before," she says. "I expected to find lewd women of low character. But a *bear*?"

She shouldn't have made the 'lewd women' remark in front of Constance, a big-boned gal who, in addition to bein' especially good at letterin', don't take to bein' called lewd in her own home. Though the *Spur* ain't technically her home, she considers it such. Had I known she was in the kitchen at the time, hearin' herself bein' called lewd, I would a' stopped what happened next before it happened. But I was already talkin' to George Murphy in the quiet corner. Actually, we hadn't begun talkin' yet, because the screamin' kept us from startin'.

By the time Wing Ding and I pulled Constance off Mrs. Plenty, we were able to count how many freckles the proper woman had on her left bosom.

Three.

But I'm the only one in the whole room that got slapped over it.

Mrs. Plenty stomped out of the saloon shoutin' somethin' about how I'd be hearin' from her attorney for an assault charge.

I look at Constance and frown.

"She started it," she says.

"You're twice her size."

"Damn right I am. Can't imagine how she managed to nurse a baby with a tit like that."

I frowned again. "I s'pect I'll have to deal with her husband, now."

"I'll deal with him if you want."

"That'd probably be best, 'less he's heeled."

She puts her hand inside her dress and fiddles around a second and produces a derringer. "Even if he is."

I sigh. "If it comes to shootin', respect the floors. They'll be yours to scrub."

"I thought Ding Dong was working here now."

"Who?"

"Ding Dong?"

"Wing Ding."

She looks confused. "Who's Ding Dong?"

"I s'pect you been workin' here long enough to know Ding Dong's the woman who does your laundry."

"Oh. Well anyway, Wing Ding is working here?"

"He is."

"Why can't he clean the floors?"

"'Cause he didn't start the fight."

"I didn't either. That bitch–"

I hate arguin' with whores. Plus, I still have five people to deal with before breakfast, and I ain't a man who likes to put off eatin' breakfast. I try to explain my logic to Constance. "If Mrs. Plenty had come in and slapped you, it'd be her fault."

"She slapped my pride."

I was about to say somethin', then realized she had a point.

"If Pete comes in, keep your mouth shut and send him my way. I'll offer him a free week of pokes."

"You'd do that?"

"I would."

Constance laughs.

"What's so funny?"

"You don't think Leah's gonna be jealous?"

"What? Why would she be jealous?"

"I'd be jealous if you were fuckin' *my* best customer for a whole week." With that, she cackles and heads back to the kitchen.

Realizin' what she said, I yell, "It wouldn't be *me* givin' the pokes, you chucklehead–"

Then I look around and see the other five grinnin' at me, 'cept for Clair Murphy, who looks like she was weaned on sour pickles. I sigh and walk back to the table.

CHAPTER 27

GEORGE MURPHY—NO relation to Clair—says the town kids keep breakin' his window and wants permission to shoot 'em in the ass with rock salt. I tell him no, since everyone knows old George is half blind.

Clair Murphy's complaint involves the half-dressed women on the balcony of Patty's Pie Palace, who make—she pauses to see if Constance is nearby before saying—"lewd noises."

"Lewd noises?"

"Yes. Every Wednesday evening, when we're walking to church."

"What sorts of lewd noises?"

"You know. Outhouse noises."

"Outhouse noises? Like what?"

Clair fixes me with a stare. "Do I *really* need to elaborate?"

I sigh. "Well ma'am, maybe them noises are actual bodily noises that ain't bein' directed at you."

"That's ridiculous. Something needs to be done. And I'll tell you something else."

I wait for her to tell me somethin' else, but she don't. So I ask, "What's that?"

"The place is called Patty's Pie Palace."

"Yes, ma'am."

"I've never seen so much as an apple pie in the front window. And if those women are baking pies for Patty, well, you'll never catch *me* serving one in polite company. While we're on the subject, you should inform Miss Patty about the ill mannered women she's hired. There are plenty of able-bodied girls in town who–why are you looking at me like that?"

"Well ma'am, there *is* no Miss Patty, and it ain't *that* kind of pie."

"What do you mean?"

"Ah, well, the name ain't got nothin' to do with bakery goods."

"Well what kind of pie are they–?" She stops in mid-sentence and makes a face like she'd swallowed some liniment after thinkin' it were candy. "That...is...the single most disgusting thing I have ever heard! You'll march over there *immediately* and make them take that sign down!"

"But ma'am,"

"Don't 'but ma'am' *me*! You're being paid to do a job and I expect you to *do* it! I want that sign torn down today, and those women flogged!"

"Flogged?"

"Publicly."

"I can't just go around floggin' women in the street."

Clair Murphy aims her evil eye at me again and says, "There's going to be hell to pay! *Hell to pay*! Do you under-*stand?*"

Before I can answer, she stomps off even angrier than Mrs. Plenty had stomped.

When she opens the front door to leave, a stick of dynamite comes flyin' in the room, hits the floor, bounces twice, and comes to a stop about six feet from the table where I'm sittin'. The fuse is short, and burnin' fast.

CHAPTER 28

I JUMP TO my feet while drawin' my gun and surprise myself by shootin' the fuse off the end of the stick just before it blows. I take a deep breath and try to cipher what just happened. Suddenly the door is kicked open and another stick of dynamite comes flyin' through. This one hits the table and bounces up. Before it hits the ground I manage to shoot the fuse off that one as well.

Furious, I holster my gun and start walkin' straight for the front door with quick steps. While I'm doin' that, nine things happen at the same time.

First, the door gets kicked open again.

Second, another stick of dynamite comes flyin' through.

Third, I catch the dynamite in my right hand and crush the fuse against my chest to snuff it out. I do all this without breakin' my stride.

Fourth, I drop the dynamite, and draw my gun, all in the same motion.

Fifth, I hear Bose Rennick's gorgeous voice on the far side of the room, behind me. "That's mighty fine shootin', Sheriff."

Sixth, I hear six clicks come from Bose's gun and wonder how he could've forgot to load it with bullets.

Seventh, without even turnin' my head, I yell, "*Rudy: Tag!*"

Eighth, I pull open the front door and see Sam Hartman standin' a few feet away, lightin' another stick of dynamite. He gives me an "Oh, shit!" look and I shoot him in the center of his chest.

Ninth, Rudy "tags" Bose so hard he slams into the wall, and hits the floor, unconscious.

As I cross the floor toward Bose, I hear the stick of dynamite explode in the street. It shatters my front door, sendin' all kinds of wood and glass splinters flyin' everywhere, but I don't so much as turn around. I just keep walkin' toward Bose, with my gun aimed on him. When I'm standin' over him, I put my gun a few inches from his head and pull the trigger.

But the only sound my gun makes is a click.

I pull the trigger again, get another click.

A gunman always knows how many bullets he's got, and I know I shot two fuses, a man, and just now, two clicks. Which means I've got another bullet in the chamber. I pull the trigger once more.

Click.

Bose comes to, and looks up at me with his terrifyin', crazy eyes. I draw back my gun, to crash it against his skull. It ain't sportin', but neither is a dynamite ambush.

I aim to kill him, once and for all.

Out of the corner of my eye I see Rose move behind me. Bose sees what I'm up to and knows he's helpless. He don't even try to speak, just closes his eyes and waits for me to bust his skull. I start to do it, but at the last possible second, Rose says somethin' that shatters everythin' I ever thought I knew or understood. I hear the words, but they make no sense.

I'm dumbstruck.

So confused am I, she has to repeat her words.

From behind me, for the second time, Rose says, "Let him go, Emmett."

I turn my head just enough to see her holdin' a gun on me.

CHAPTER 29

"ROSE?"

She steps past me and hits Bose over the head with her gun. It wasn't a skull-smashin' hit, more of a tap, just enough to knock him unconscious again. Then she says, "We need to get him out of here."

"I aim to kill him."

"No."

"What do you mean, no?"

"I won't let you kill him."

"Why?"

She says, "It's too late. They're coming."

"Who?"

She nods to the area where my door used to be. "The whole town."

Rose is right. Within seconds there's thirty people pushin' through the front openin'. I give Rose an angry look.

look. Thanks to her, I lost my one opportunity to murder Bose Rennick in cold blood.

Within moments the town wants to lynch him. I'd be one of 'em sayin' the same thing, 'cept for this cloth badge in my pocket. The badge changes everythin'. I don't know the law as well as some, but I know the badge won't let me hang a man without a trial. I find myself havin' to protect the very man I would a' killed a minute earlier if I hadn't been interrupted.

A lot of things that happened tonight don't make sense. Like how come Bose's gun didn't fire six straight times? And how could mine misfire three? In my entire life—even with wet ammunition—I never saw six, or even three straight misfires. And both at the same time? Impossible. And why wouldn't Rose let me kill him? And what happened to Gentry and Wing Ding? They were both in the kitchen when Bose came through. How could they not have seen him, or remained quiet when I started shootin' in the very next room? Or when the dynamite went off right outside the door? And how could Bose walk right past Rudy without seein' him? Like I say, it don't make sense.

And now, suddenly, Gentry's by my side, and Wing is helpin' me drag Bose Rennick to my indoor jail hole. Who'd a' thought he'd be my first prisoner? I'm not happy about him bein' alive, but the good news is, he ain't goin' anywhere, and he'll be easy to convict.

Before tossin' him in the hole, we clean out his pockets and find a knife, two derringers, sixteen bullets and eighty-eight dollars. After lockin' him up, we go out front to search Sam Hartman's pockets, but learn there ain't enough of Sam to search. After a few minutes we're able to find a few chunks of him, and Wing says his uncle will bury Sam's bones for free if his hogs can eat the meat off 'em. That sounds like a fair trade to me, and when no one objects, that's what we do.

I hire several men to help us clean the main room of the *Spur*. I can't patch the door till the lumber shipment arrives from St. Joe tomorrow, so that's an issue. Another is Rose. I can't find a private place to talk to her, so I ask her to come with me to Shrug's room. When we get there, somethin' else ain't right.

"Where's Shrug?"

"He left before they got here."

"When?"

"While you were talking to the Murphys."

I frown. "Did you see him leave?"

"What difference does it make?"

"Well, is he okay?"

"He's fine. I made him go."

"Why?"

"I was afraid he'd kill Bose to protect you."

"Where did he go?"

She looks up at the ceilin'.

"What," I say. "On the roof?"

"In the attic."

"He's in the attic now?"

Rose shrugs.

"Why can't I hear him?"

She smiles.

"What happened to Gentry?" I say.

"I cleared her head."

"What the hell does that mean?"

"It's like she's awake, but sleeping."

"And Bose?"

"I felt him coming, and fixed it so he couldn't see me, Wing, Gentry or Rudy."

"You fixed it."

"Right."

"And his gun?"

"I fixed that, too."

"And mine?"

"Yes."

"But you let me shoot the first three shots."

"I did."

"You let me kill Sam Hartman."

"Yes."

"But not Bose."

She says nothin' in reply.

I stare at her for a long time without speakin'. Finally I say, "I've known you for years."

"Yes."

I take a deep breath, let it out slowly. "You owe me an explanation, Rose."

She nods.

"Well?"

"It's hard to explain. I'm not sure where to start."

"Start at the beginnin'."

"That's too much to tell."

"Then tell me this. Why did you stop me from killin' Bose Rennick?"

Rose is a beautiful woman. Her hair is black as coal, and her eyes change dependin' on what she wears. Right now they're the color of an almond husk, with a light green tinge around the circle in the center. Her skin is milky white and never darkens, even after months outdoors in the sun. She's slight in size, though well-conformed and proportional. Her hips ain't suited to birthin', but still manage to draw admirin' glances from men and women alike. I notice all this about her 'cause there ain't much else to do till she answers my question.

Which she finally does.

"You and Bose are linked together," she says.

"We're *what?*"

"Linked. Your destinies. You're tied together in life."

"By what?"

"Common purpose."

"Which is?"

"That I can't tell you."

"Well, you ain't told me nothin' then, have you?"

I can tell she's strugglin' to think of a way to tell me somethin', without tellin' me everythin'.

She bites the corner of her lower lip and starts over.

CHAPTER 30

"EVERYONE HAS A purpose in life," Rose says.

"What's mine?"

"To live awhile longer."

"Why?"

"That I can't–"

"Right. You can't tell me."

She says, "I have a purpose, too."

"Can you tell me that?"

"I can tell you some."

"Go ahead, then."

She moves to the bed Shrug had been recuperatin' in, and sits on the side. Then brushes a strand of hair from her eyes and tucks it behind her ear to hold it in place. She says, "I've lived a lot of years, and I'll live a lot more. And while I'm alive, I'm tied to a certain lineage of humanity."

"I don't have any idea what you're sayin'."

"I know."

I sigh. "Am I just stupid?"

She smiles. "Not at all. It's my fault, not yours. I'm a protector. I protect a certain line of people."

"Go on."

"Pretend I age one year for every ten that other people age."

"*What?*"

"Just pretend. It'll make it easier for me to explain."

"If you explain much more, I might have to put you in a crazy home."

"You'll put me in no such place!"

"I was joshin'. But I don't approve of the tone you just used."

"You'll get that tone again if you talk about putting me away. You have no idea what being locked away is like."

"I once spent three days and nights in a leaky jail hole in January!"

"The suffering you've experienced in life is like eating a sugar cookie."

I frown at her. "A sugar cookie."

"That's right."

"Fine. Forget I said it then. I'm still peeved about this business with Bose Rennick."

"Fine," Rose says. "Now pay attention, because I don't think I can say this twice."

"Okay."

"Don't try to believe me, or argue with me, just hear me out."

"Okay."

"If Bose Rennick dies, you die."

"*What*? That's ridiculous."

"Emmett?"

"Sorry. Go on."

"I can't allow you to die, and can't allow Bose to die."

"Then why ain't you followin' him?"

"Because I didn't realize who your link was until last fall."

"When he ambushed us on the trail?"

"That's right."

"And somehow you knew he and I were tied up together."

"Yes."

"And you're protectin' us."

"Yes."

"But you ain't been here since October. And you ain't been followin' Bose around, as far as I can tell."

She's quiet, waitin' to see if I can figure it out. I think on it a minute and say, "Are you tellin' me the only way Bose and I are gonna die is if one of us kills the other?"

"Yes."

"So if Bose ain't around, I've got nothin' to worry about?"

"That's generally true."

"Generally?"

"You could die at any time."

"But if I do, Bose dies?"

"That's right."

"Then I don't understand. If you're protectin' us, why ain't you *protectin'* us?"

"Because I have a life, too. And my vision is that one of you kills the other."

"But you could be wrong?"

"I could be."

"Which of us kills the other?"

"In my vision?"

"Uh huh."

"I can't tell you."

"Just say if it's me. I hate that silky-voiced bastard."

"We're getting off track here."

I frown again. "I guess there's some satisfaction that if he kills me, he has to die too."

She nods.

"How long do I have?"

"What do you mean?"

"After I lynch Bose, how long before I die?"

She pats my leg. "You're not going to lynch Bose."

"Oh, really?"

"Really."

"And why's that?"

"Because you're going to help him escape."

CHAPTER 31

"YOU MUST BE crazy if you think I'm gonna help Bose Rennick escape from my jail. Why, I'd be the laughin' stock of the town. After all that time I put in, and all that talk I done about it? There's no way!"

"You *will* let him escape. We just have to figure out how."

"Give me one good reason why I should."

"Gentry. Because you'll die three days after he does."

"First of all, I don't believe a word of this destiny thing. Him gettin' lynched can't cause my death. That's just mumbo-jumbo. Not only that, you might be off on your three days."

"Just...pretend it's true for a minute, and pretend I'm trying to save your life."

I take a deep breath while rememberin' Rose has saved my life several times in the past.

"Okay."

"How can you help him escape?" she asks.

"Guess I'd just open the hatch and let him run off."

"He aims to kill you, Emmett. He's not going to rest until he does."

"What if you told him the same thing you told me? That we're linked by destiny."

"You know Bose pretty well, don't you?"

"I know him some."

"Do you think he'd believe that?"

"I don't know. He was there when you spooked his horse last fall. He was here today when his gun didn't work."

"Trust me. He'll kill you in a heartbeat, now that he knows where you live."

I pause a minute. Then say, "Supposin' you're right about Bose and me. How long are you gonna protect us from each other?"

"Until the big event."

"The big event."

"That's right."

"And what's that?"

"I can't tell you."

"Of course you can't. But since you're the only one who had a vision, and since you won't share it, you're gonna have to come up with the plan for how to keep him from killin' me after we let him go."

She nods. "Fair enough."

"You got a plan?"

"Not yet, but I'll work on it."

"Well, you better be quick, 'cause that bunch downstairs wants blood."

"I know."

I turn to leave the room. She stops me by sayin', "Emmett?"

"Yeah?"

"That was a brilliant piece of shooting you did today."

I search her face to see if she's makin' fun of me. She don't appear to be.

"At first I thought it was me doin' the shootin'. Then I figured it must a' been you."

"It was you, Emmett. You're the most amazing gunman who's ever lived."

"That you know of."

"Trust me, Emmett. You're the best."

"What about Bad Vlad?"

"Not even close."

"And Bose Rennick?"

"Very close."

"He's that good?"

She nods.

"I never seen him draw and shoot."

"He drew and shot today, after coming in the back of the saloon."

I think about how I heard his voice and then six clicks. He must a' drawn and shot after speakin', which was a split second later.

"How come he's got such a beautiful speakin' voice?"

She shrugs. "It's his other gift. Everyone gets at least two, in my experience."

"What's Gentry's? Besides beauty?"

"Her other gift is you."

"Really?"

She nods.

"What's my other gift? Besides bein' a good shooter?"

"It'll sound silly to you."

"Tell me anyway."

She fixes her eyes on mine. Then, without crackin' a smile, says, "A heart that's true."

CHAPTER 32

"HEARD YOU GOT eighty-eight dollars off Bose Rennick," Mayor Ha-a-a-averhouse says.

"Word travels fast."

"I'm two doors down."

"Right."

"Forty-four of that goes to the Town Council," he says.

"Minus his burial fee."

"Thirty-nine, then."

The tiny Mayor looks twice as small standin' between Bob Robert, who must certainly be the world's tallest man, and Harry Haverhouse, the world's widest.

"What about the damage to my store?" I say.

"Sam Hartman owes you for that."

I frown. "Do you three always travel together?"

"What three?"

I count out thirty-nine dollars and hand it to him.

He gives thirteen each to Bob and Harry. Then says, "What I'm about to ask is meant as a compliment."

"Ask it then."

He puts three dollars in his pocket and holds the other ten where I can see it. Then says, "Is Gentry still taking customers?"

I try to keep the edge outta my voice, and the steel outta my stare when I say "No." But he can tell I'm simmerin' inside.

"Relax, Sheriff. It was a fair question, and now I've got my answer."

It was a fair question, given Gentry's history. But that don't mean I approve of it.

Mayor Ha-a-a-averhouse says, "We're gentlemen here, there's no cause to be insulted. The subject will never come up again. You have my word."

I nod. "See that it don't."

The little man smiles what I take to be a genuinely warm smile. "I'm very happy for you," he says. "Gentry's clearly a wonderful woman. I'd even go so far as to say she's a one-in-a-million. Please accept my apology."

He bows.

It were a hell of an apology. I had to take it.

"Fair enough," I say. "Bygones."

I notice he's still holding the ten dollars out. "Somethin' else I can do for you?"

"Another question," he says.

"Ask it."

"What about the bear?"

"Rudy?"

"Yes."

"What about him?"

He waves the ten dollars and licks his lips.

What he's askin for don't sink into my brain immediately, but when it does I give him a double look and start rollin' up my sleeves. I don't care how short, tall, and wide these circus folk are. You don't come into my place and ask to fuck my woman and my bear in the same conversation.

The Mayor gets a frightened look on his face and starts movin' away at a quick pace. "Let me know if you recover any money from Hartman!" he calls over his shoulder.

Gentry comes up behind me and puts her hand on my shoulder.

"You okay, honey?"

"Them fellers got me riled."

"I can tell. You were rolling up your sleeves. I was worried."

"Well, everythin's fine. For now. But you need to stay away from them fellers."

"Are they dangerous?"

"I don't think so. But they're mighty disgustin'. At least the Mayor is."

"What did he want?"

"You wouldn't believe me if I told you."

"I've seen and heard a lot in my seventeen years."

"You ain't heard this."

"Try me."

"He wants to poke the bear."

She cocks her head. "By poke, you don't mean..."

"I do."

Gentry ain't as disgusted as I figured she'd be. In fact, she starts laughin'.

"You think that's *funny?*"

"Just the picture it puts in my head," she says. Then laughs again, harder.

"What now?"

"I was picturing it going the other way."

"What other way?"

She giggles. "Rudy poking the Mayor."

"*What?*"

She laughs again.

I try not to think about it, but now she's put the picture in my head and I can't shake it out. I don't laugh with her, 'cause it's Rudy we're talkin' about.

But I can't help smilin'.

CHAPTER 33

"HEY, SUGAR, HOW about standin' over the top of these boards so I can look up your dress!"

Bose Rennick has come to and is watchin' Rose through the wooden slats. She's sittin' at the kitchen table, drinkin' tea. He moves around a little, to get a better look. Then says, "Say, I know you! You're that bitch who spooked our horses a few months back. How'd you do that, pretty lady?"

Me and Gentry are hearin' all this from the other side of the kitchen table where he can't see us. I'm checkin' the bullets from my gun belt carefully, and loadin' 'em in my gun. One thing about Bose, he's got a voice to warm the devil's heart. It's a thing of beauty. So deep, rich, and clear it is, I imagine he could make a fortune singin' in opry houses back east. Not that I ever been in one. But that's the kind of voice them fellers probably have.

Bose starts up on Rose again. "I didn't mean to call you a bad name, Sugar Britches. I'm right sorry I said that. Don't know what happened to my manners just now. Maybe it's 'cause you smacked me over the head with a gun awhile ago. But I don't hold you personally accountable. Although I'd *love* to *hold* you!"

Bose continues with that luscious voice of his, tellin' Rose what he'd do with her once he got her naked. Gentry keeps grinnin' at Rose, and raisin' her eyebrows, and I have to say, the idea of someone doin' any a' them things to Rose is funny to think about, 'cause I never knowed her to be anythin' but a very proper young lady. On the other hand, she appears to be twenty and claims to have buried six husbands. I have to think them husbands were dead when she buried them, and if so, it crosses my mind for the first time to wonder if she might a' wore some of 'em out under the bed sheets!

Though Gentry and me are grinnin' at Rose through all this nasty talk, she's thinkin' other thoughts about how to set him free and keep him away from me, at least till our common purpose thing has happened.

She motions me and Gentry to follow her into the main room, and we do. She picks out the far table, the most secluded one where I'd listened to the Murphys tell me how to sheriff earlier. Rose hadn't wanted to include Gentry in the scheme, but I insisted. I have too much pride to let Gentry think I lost a prisoner after spendin' all that time buildin' the jail hole. Plus, if I put another prisoner in there, she'd never be able to sleep at night if she thought he could escape. I explained all this to Rose, and she agreed to involve Gentry in the discussions.

"Any ideas?" Rose says.

"What if you cut his arms off?" Gentry says.

"Excuse me?"

"If Emmett cut his arms off, he wouldn't be able to shoot. Wait. You could probably just cut his hands off and get the same benefit."

Rose looks at me like she might be concerned for my safety.

"What?" Gentry says.

"He needs to be able to defend himself," Rose says. "He needs to live. We're just trying to keep him from killing Emmett."

"What if you broke his gun hand? Then he'd have to teach himself to shoot left-handed."

I look at Rose.

She says, "That's more humane. But he shoots quite well with both hands. He might still come after Emmett. And a broken hand wouldn't prevent him from using a shotgun or rifle."

"What if we train him like they trained Rudy?" Gentry says.

She's beginnin' to amaze me with how many ideas she can come up with to disable a gunman.

"What," I say. "Put a rope through Bose's nose? I'd like that!"

Rose frowns at me.

Gentry says, "No. I'm talking about conditioning him. That's what Sergio called it when they trained Rudy. He said they conditioned him to dance when the music was played."

"Tell me your idea," Rose says.

"Well, say we turn Bose loose five miles away. Shrug can be out there in the dark. If Bose starts heading toward Dodge, Shrug can chunk a rock and smash his head. Not enough to kill him, but enough to hurt him. Then, when he gets up again, if he starts heading toward Dodge again, Shrug would hit him again. Bose wouldn't know where the rocks were coming from, but after a few days of this, he'd be conditioned not to head toward Dodge."

I look at her like it's not much of an idea, but Rose surprises me by sayin', "Not bad, Gentry. That could actually work."

Gentry beams.

Rose continues, "But it's probably not a good long-term idea, because the conditioning might take weeks or months, and it's not fair to poor Wayne to make him do that. Or to be responsible if something goes wrong."

"What could go wrong?" Gentry says.

"He was shot in the shoulder. He won't be able to throw as hard or accurately as he used to, at least, not for awhile. He might kill Bose by mistake. Or have to get close enough to where Bose could just start shooting in a circle. If that happens, Wayne could get shot again."

"Wow, you're right," Gentry says. "Can we cut his pecker off?"

I say, "How's that gonna help?"

"It'll make every woman in the west feel safer."

Rose shakes her head and says, "No. I need him to survive. And I *especially* need his pecker."

I almost fall out of my chair.

Gentry gives her a double look, smiles, and says, "*Rose*?"

Rose gives us a confused look, then realizes what she'd said. Then she does somethin' I only seen her do a few times in all the years I've known her.

She laughs.

"Oh, my!" she says. "I didn't mean it *that* way! What I meant was...oh, never mind!" She laughs again.

And we laugh with her.

"I'm Hollis Williams!" someone shouts from outside the *Spur*. "Where's the Sheriff?"

Hollis Williams stomps through the wide hole that used to be my front door. He pauses to frown at the shot up piano, looks across the room at Rudy and instinctively puts his hand on the gun handle in his holster. He decides Rudy's not a threat at the moment, spies me, and stomps right up to our table. With each right step, his spurs jingle. With each left, they jangle. His walk is quite musical, and Rudy thinks so, too, because he starts dancin'.

"Stop right there!" I holler.

He does.

"Turn sideways."

He frowns. Hollis looks like a man used to givin' orders, not takin' 'em. But he's never seen a gun go from a holster to a man's hand as fast as mine just did, and he's in shock. Though he's unhappy about bein' ordered, he does what I say.

Before he finishes turnin', I fire two quick shots and his spurs go flyin' across the floor. I twirl my gun, put the barrel near my mouth and blow the smoke away, like the eastern dandy did in a stage show me and Gentry saw in Wichita one night. Then I put the gun back in my holster with a flourish, same way the dandy did, and Gentry grins at me and claps her hands.

Rose rolls her eyes.

Hollis scowls me with an angry sneer to show me he's the kind of man who makes his own rules. I can tell he's wealthy by his clothes and his manner. He also strikes me as the type of man who might be willin' to flog Patti's whores in the middle of the street if it suits him. He takes a deep breath to puff himself up to full size, and says, "You the Sheriff?"

"I am. But I'm talkin' to these ladies at the moment."

"Well, I've rode eight hours to see you, and you can either pour me a whiskey or take my meetin' now. I've got a serious complaint to file, and I'm a busy man."

"We're all busy," I say, noddin' at the fellers I've paid to finish cleanin' up the main room so I can open my card tables for business.

"You don't look busy to me."

"Is that what you came to talk about? Whether I'm busy enough to suit you?"

"In part. And you should take a better tone of respect with me. I'm a man of influence."

"With who?"

He shows me a self-satisfied smirk and says, "The Governor."

"Meanin'?"

"You want to keep that badge, you'll get your ass in motion and do your job."

"Well, I just killed Sam Hartman and locked up Bose Rennick."

"So?"

"I 'spect the Governor would call that a good day's work."

"Sheriffin' ain't about what you did earlier today. It's about what you do next."

"Do tell."

"We can talk in front of these women, or we can talk alone. Your choice. Either way, you'll pay me for them spurs."

"You saw the sign on the piano. No music allowed."

"I didn't play the fargin' piano. I was wearin' spurs."

"Those were musical spurs if I ever heard any. They were like tiny cymbals. You can take 'em with you when you leave."

Rose and Gentry can tell my fuse is lit. For the safety of this rude man of influence, Gentry says, "Rose, let's go up to Shrug's room and keep our conversation going. I have lots of ideas."

She nods, and they get up to leave.

CHAPTER 34

HOLLIS AND I watch the ladies go up the stairs. Then he says, "Someone shot and butchered one a' my cows."

"I'm sorry to hear that."

"Sorry don't cut it. I want you to ride out to my place, find out who done it, and arrest him. Or them."

I take my hat off, smooth my hair down, then put my hat back on, and shape it some.

"Your spread's an eight-hour ride?"

"That's right. And it takes four hours to cross, from one end to the other."

"And how many cows you got?"

"About sixteen thousand."

"About?"

"That's right."

"Might you have sixteen thousand and three?"

"I *might* have sixteen thousand three hundred. What's your point?"

"My point is, you could lose three hundred cows and not know the difference. Why come all this way for one cow that some hungry feller probably ate to survive?"

Hollis Williams jumps to his feet.

"Is that the type of attitude we're to expect from you as a sheriff?"

"Let me think on that a minute," I say, reviewin' the words I'd spoke. After doin' that a minute, I get up from the table, walk to the bar, remove a good bottle of whiskey from under the counter, bring it back and hand it to him.

"Yes," I say.

"Yes, what?"

"That's the type of attitude you can expect from me about wastin' what could amount to days or weeks of my time over one cow from a herd that's so big you can't even count it. The whiskey's to let you know I'm sorry about your cow. I hope it brings you comfort on your long ride back."

"That's it?"

"No, there's one more thing."

He don't speak, so I say, "If you ever come across the person who butchered that cow, I hope you'll be charitable toward him."

The red creeps from his neck into his face. A vein on the side of his head, just below his ear, looks like it's about to bust.

"You can bet this ain't over!" he snarls.

"Well, I'm sorry to hear that."

He grabs his whiskey and stomps off the same way he stomped in, except that his spurs ain't makin' music. When he gets to the front, he suddenly remembers the spurs, turns, and walks back to retrieve 'em. He puts 'em in his pocket, gives me one last scowl, and leaves.

I'd sheriffed once before, but back in them days, people didn't have time for these sorts of problems. I ain't sure this type of sherrifin' suits me.

I head up the stairs, knock on the guest room where Shrug had slept. Gentry opens the door and beckons me in. Then closes it behind me, and sits on the bed next to Rose.

Rose says, "Gentry and I came up with an idea, but I need to ask you a question."

"Go ahead."

"Are gunfighters superstitious?"

"Very."

"You think Bose is?"

"I'd count on it. Why?"

"If we could make him believe his bullets won't work in Kansas, would he stay away?"

"Well, he misfired six times in a row. But he might be inclined to blame the gun or bullets before blamin' the state of Kansas."

"But if we plant the idea in his head," Gentry says, "maybe we could condition his mind to believe it."

"He'd need more proof."

Rose says, "I aim to give him plenty."

"You gonna put a spell on his gun?"

"Do I look like like a witch to you?"

I look at Gentry. She mouths the word *Yes!*

I smile at her, but direct my answer to Rose.

"I don't know enough about witchery to say. But I had three perfectly good bullets in my gun that didn't work awhile ago, and that ain't never happened before. Nor have I ever known a gunfighter like Bose to have six straight misfires."

"So if Bose had thirty or forty straight misfires, with different guns, what would he think?"

"He ain't likely to blame Kansas, no matter how much proof you give him."

Rose says, "But if we put enough doubt in his mind, would he feel *unlucky* in Kansas?"

"If he's superstitious enough, and has enough proof, he might not want to rely on usin' a fire arm in Kansas, but I reckon he'll cross the border and take a few shots from time to time to see if it's really true."

The ladies look at each other.

Rose says, "What do you think?"

Gentry says, "I think it's worth a try."

They look at me and I say, "What've you got in mind?"

CHAPTER 35

WE ALL GO downstairs together, past the few men who just came in lookin' to play cards. Leah and Hester are standin' with 'em, takin' drink orders, tryin' to talk 'em into goin' upstairs now and playin' cards later. Rose enters the kitchen alone. Gentry and me listen from just outside the doorway, out of sight. Wing sees us from the other side of the kitchen, by the back door, where he's standin' guard with a shotgun. I put my finger to my lips so he won't speak. Rose walks over to the table where Bose can see her from inside the hole.

"Well, hi there, Sugar Britches," Bose says with a voice bathed in honey. What would it take to get you to just stand over the top of these boards?"

"Maybe if you rip your eyes out of their sockets," she answers, sweetly.

"It's a deal! Come on!"

"You first," she says.

"Oh, what I'd give to get inside your drawers!" he says. "I bet you got *fire* in them britches!"

"You have no idea."

"How about you slide that bolt and let me out of here?"

"If I did, what would you do?"

"Anythin' you want."

"Would you kill yourself?"

"Why, sure I would! Just get my gun and slide the bolt. If you want me dead, you can pull the trigger yourself."

"It wouldn't matter," Rose says.

"What wouldn't?"

"I couldn't shoot you."

"'Cause you got feelins' for me? Is that why you didn't let Emmett shoot me awhile ago?"

"I *do* have feelings for you, Bose. But all of them are bad."

"Aw, you don't mean that."

"What I mean to say is, your bullets won't work in Kansas."

"Excuse me?"

"It's a fact."

"If it's a fact, you shouldn't mind lettin' me have my gun."

"I don't mind."

"Really? You'd give me my gun?"

"I might."

"Don't tease me, sugar. Them townies are gonna come for me in a couple hours. That's how it works. They're off somewhere, drinkin' up some courage. In the end, Emmett'll stand aside and let 'em take me. I'm as good as hung if I can't defend myself."

"You'll never be able to defend yourself. Not in Kansas."

"Why not?"

I walk in and say, "Because she's a witch. And she put a spell on you, just like she put a spell on your horses last fall, when you got the drop on us near Copper Lake."

I close the kitchen door so Gentry can guard it from the main room.

Bose says, "There's no such thing as witches."

"Then you and your men must be the worst horsemen in the world."

"That was some sort of fluke," he says.

"You think?"

"I know."

I tell Rose to fetch me Bose's gun and gun belt. "Wing? Come here and lift the lid."

Bose suddenly gets nervous. "What're you up to, Emmett?"

"I'm gonna give you your gun."

"Bullshit."

I nod at Wing. He slides the bolt and lifts the floor boards up and swings them all the way back. The only thing between us and Bose is the second set of wooden slats. I nod and Wing unlocks that hatch, too, then lifts it out of the way. Now Bose's head is about two feet from our boots. Rose tosses him his gun belt and holster. He can see his gun in the holster.

"You're gonna shoot me and pretend I'm tryin' to escape!" he says.

I point to my gun. It's in my holster. I put my hands up.

"Shoot me," I say.

I'll give Bose credit for one thing. He can recognize an opportunity when he sees it. Before I got the words completely out of my mouth, he pulls his gun and makes it click three times. He frowns and checks to see if there are bullets in it.

"What've you done to my gun?"

"Nothin'."

"You've ruined my bullets somehow!"

"Nope."

Bose tries to fire three more times, turns the gun sideways, pops the cylinder, lets the bullets slide out, pulls six more from his gunbelt, takes careful aim, and pulls the trigger six times.

And gets six clicks.

"This is *bullshit!*" he says. But he holsters his gun and straps on his gun belt anyway.

"Try mine," I say, tossin' him my gun.

He catches it, turns it toward me and pulls the trigger.

Click. Click. Click.

"You think that's funny?" he says.

"I do. Toss it back and I'll show you how funny it is."

He tosses it back and I shoot a hole in the bottom of his holster. The sound is deafening. We hear Gentry outside the door, tellin' the folks in the main room, "Don't worry, Emmett's just shootin' a rat. A small one," she adds, "Not Bose Rennick."

I hear the customers laugh. If Bose is right, and a bunch of men come for him in a little while, these men won't be a party to it. They're steady customers.

I toss my gun back to Bose.

"You try it," I say.

He does. And gets two more clicks.

"Reload it with your bullets," I say.

He does.

"Shoot me a couple times."

He shoots twice.

Click. Click.

I hold out my hand. He frowns and tosses me the gun. I shoot his gunbelt again.

"Another rat!" Gentry calls out.

"Remind me not to order supper!" one of the customers shouts back, which causes a loud roar of laughter from the others in there.

The customers ain't worried, since Gentry ain't.

I toss the gun back to Bose. He tries to shoot it again, gets another click for his trouble. Then tosses it back to me.

"I don't know what type of trick you're playin'," he says, "but I ain't buyin' she's a witch."

"Wing," I say. "Toss him the shotgun."

He does. Bose turns it on me, cocks one of the barrels, pulls the trigger.

Click.

He opens the action to see two shells inside, shuts it, cocks the second barrel, and pulls that trigger.

Click.

"Toss him two more shells," I say to Wing.

He pulls two shells from his pocket and tosses 'em to Bose.

"Load 'em both, but just shoot one," I say.

He does, and gets a click.

I reach for the shotgun and he hands it over.

"You ain't gonna shoot my gun belt with that thing, are you?"

"Do you think this barrel will fire?"

He nods.

"How many bullets you need in your gun belt?" I ask.

He counts. "Eighteen."

I fetch a box of bullets from one of the kitchen drawers and toss it to him. "Load it."

"Why?"

"We're gonna let you escape."

"Why?"

"What do you care?"

He shrugs. "You're right. I don't care."

CHAPTER 36

NO ONE'S EXPECTIN' us to let Bose go, partic'larly in broad daylight, so we check out back and, sure enough, there's no one out there. I tell Bose to leave his hat in the hole. Few folks have seen his face, but his hat's distictive.

"How about I carry my hat?" he says.

I don't blame him. In the same situation, I'd want mine. It's harder to break in a new hat than a new horse. Which reminds me of somethin' I need to tell Bose.

"I can't return your money or your horse. But the two finest horses I ever seen are saddled up and tied to the post behind my store. Pick one and ride off."

"Ain't you worried I'll shoot you?"

"Accordin' to my witch, you can't shoot nothin' in Kansas. And I believe her. Before you climb out, pick up all them bullets you dropped and hand 'em to me."

When all the bullets are accounted for, Wing drops the bucket in the hole. Bose turns it upside down, stands on it, and climbs out of the jail hole.

"I appreciate you doin' this for me," he says. "I won't forget it. You and me are square after his." He winks one of those god-awful eyes at me, and I nod.

"I'm glad to hear that, Bose."

"You've got my word," he says.

"That means a lot."

I still can't get over his voice. So special is it, if he told me to go to hell, I'd actually look forward to the trip.

"When you walk out of here, move slowly," I say, "so as not to draw any attention to yourself."

Bose hesitates at the back door, looks around, and walks out. He chooses one of the horses, climbes on its back, and heads away, at a steady walk.

Rose, Wing and I sit at the kitchen table. We aim to give Bose enough time to make a clean getaway, so Wing and I fill the time by checkin' our guns and ammunition. Suddenly, I hear four clicks behind me, and turn to see Bose Rennick aimin' a gun at my back. He grins and says, "Can't blame a guy for tryin'!" Then he says to Rose, "Last chance to come with me, Sugar Britches!"

From somewhere–who knows where–Rose flings two rats at Bose. He fires two clicks that no doubt would a' hit both of 'em in mid air, had the bullets worked.

Wing lifts his shotgun and cocks one of the barrels, and Bose takes off.

Then I say to Rose, "Sugar Britches, are you certain Bose is part of my destiny?"

Wing laughs out loud. Rose says, "I know it's hard to believe, but yes. And Emmett?"

"Yeah?"

"If you call me Sugar Britches again, you'll wish you hadn't."

"Okay. Sorry."

She looks at Wing, implyin' the same thing. He nods and mutters somethin' in Chinese that makes Rose's eyes go wide. When Rose answers him in Chinese, Wing's eyes grow twice as wide. He jumps on the floor and lays himself full-length, face down, while shakin' all his limbs and makin' all sorts of babblin' sounds.

"What's he doin'?" I say.

"Begging my forgiveness for what he just said about me."

"In Chinese?"

"Mandarin."

"Can you let him up? I'm sure he didn't mean it."

"He meant it all right."

"How bad could it be?"

"We don't have words for it in English."

"Wing! Why would you speak like that to Rose?"

"I not know she understand. I act brave. In my culture woman not speak down to man. Not mean what I say."

I look at Rose. "We got more important things to do."

She says somethin' to him in Chinese or Mandarin or whatever the hell they speak. He says somethin' back, gets up, says somethin' else, and bows deeply to Rose. She says somethin' else, and he nods and runs out the back door to the out house.

"Is everythin' worked out?" I say.

"Yes."

"Then why's he so upset?"

"I forgave him, but told him to sleep alone tonight, and have a large bucket of water handy."

"Why?"

"Because at some point in the middle of the night, his private parts are going to burst into flames."

"You'd do that?"

"Of course not. But *he* will."

"I don't understand."

"I plant the seed. His mind does the rest."

"So when his privates burst into flame it's all in his mind?"

"Yes."

"So it's not really happening?"

"Of *course* it's happening! It's just happening in his mind."

She sees I'm confused, and adds, "That's where all the real things happen, Emmett. It's where the pain is."

"In the mind?"

"Exactly."

"What about Bose?"

"What about him?"

"How long is the spell on him gonna last?"

"What spell?"

For the hundredth time since I've known Rose, I find myself wonderin' how much I know and how much I dreamt about somethin' that just happened. I wonder if somethin' happened, or nothin' happened, or if whatever happened was only in my mind. I give up wonderin' about it, and go to the back door to whistle the sound a wood warbler makes. When Shrug shows up I ask him how he's feelin'. He hits his hurt shoulder and grins. Then winks at Rose, and she gives him some sort of secret smile.

To Shrug I say, "If you're willin', I'd like to lock you in my jail hole."

Shrug shuffles to the jail hole, looks down into it a second, then hops in.

I stand over him and look down. "You need anythin'?"

He shakes his head.

A very shaken and humbled Wing Ding comes back inside and helps me lock both of the wooden doors above Shrug's head. Then I get one of the chairs, put it on top of the hinged floorboards, and have Wing sit there, holdin' his shotgun.

Then Rose, Gentry, and I go back into the main room, where I see a line of people at the far side near the quiet table, waitin' to talk to the Sheriff.

Rose says, "I'll move my things into Wayne's room."

Gentry says, "I'll tend bar awhile."

I kiss Gentry and head over to my sheriffin' table.

CHAPTER 37

MAVIS BEECHUM IS upset her layin' hen went missin'. Bill Hardy wants to register an assault charge against Gideon Rigby for givin' him a black eye. Two angry neighbors want me to ride out to their place to make a rulin' on a fence line. I decide to go with 'em, since it ain't far, and because it'll help establish my alibi when the town discovers Bose Rennick has escaped.

I tell the rest of the complainers I'll be back in an hour. I also ask someone to volunteer to sit in the kitchen with Wing Ding till I get back. One of the card table groups says they'll all go in there and sit if they can play cards and drink some free whiskey. I offer 'em a bottle, and they move their game into the kitchen.

"Leave the main door open, boys!" I call to 'em, so everyone from the main room can walk in and out as they please. The more activity, the better the alibi.

When I get back from rulin' on the fence line, I find a small mob in the main room.

"Where you been?" Ben Dover yells.

There's probably twenty of 'em, and a half-dozen more in the kitchen. Some of my regular customers walk over and stand next to me.

"I appreciate that," I say, "But I'm no longer sheriff." I take the cloth badge out of my pocket and hand it to Ben, who appears to be leadin' the mob.

"I ain't takin' this," Ben says. "But we aim to take your prisoner and hang him."

"Take him then," I say, "but it's on you when the Marshall shows up and asks about it."

"I reckon he'll blame you," Ben says.

"Not if I ain't the sheriff."

"Where's the Mayor?" Ben says.

Everyone looks around, but no one sees him.

Ben frowns and says, "I reckon the Marshall and Governor can't punish the entire town. Plus, there's no judge to hear the case anyway."

We all stand there a minute, and Ben says, "What if we open the hatch and let him try to escape?"

"If you're gonna gun him down, make sure he's outdoors first," I say.

"Done."

He turns to the mob and shouts, "How about it, are you with me?"

They all let out a hoo-raw.

"Okay then, let's get him!"

They open the hatches and see nothin', 'cept a small area under the second hatch that's been dug away. Ben makes all the shocked noises you'd expect him to make, then gets on his hands and knees and looks into the hole, where the earth has been dug away, and follows the path with his eyes.

Ben says, "Best I can tell, he's dug himself out and traveled under the floor, toward the back. Some of you need to go outside and see if there's a hole where he's busted out. If not, he's still under the foundation somewhere!"

Within seconds someone finds the hole Shrug kicked open when he broke out.

Forty men are now lookin' around in the open area behind the buildin'. One of 'em yells, "There's someone hidin' in the out house."

Ben Dover rushes over and yells, "You inside the shit house! Come out right now!"

From inside, a huge voice roars back, "Stand back, or you'll wish you had!"

"That's Bose Rennick's voice!" someone shouts. "I'd recognize it anywhere!"

The crowd begins shooting into the out house from all angles. They fire about fifty rounds before Ben gets them to stop.

"He's either dead by now, or jumped into the shit hole," he says.

Someone kicks the door open and tentatively looks down into the shit hole. "He's in there all right, but it ain't Bose Rennick!"

"Well, who the hell is it?" Ben yells.

CHAPTER 38

BY THE TIME we get the Mayor out, half the crowd is angry, the other half is laughin' their asses off, but all are thirsty. We head back into my saloon and do a banner night, till someone gets the idea in their head to organize a posse. Someone else tells 'em he's done posse work before and it was a big waste of time. They come to the conclusion there's more to be gained by whorin' and drinkin', which is music to any saloon keeper's ears.

But someone else has been thinkin' things through and remembers me firin' two shots a few hours ago, while Bose was still under my care. I notice Rose is on the balcony, lookin' down on the proceedin's. Gentry's standin' next to her, lookin' very nervous.

Ben Dover stands up on his chair to publicly confront me. When he speaks, the crowd quiets down.

"What about them rats, Emmett?"

"What rats?"

"The ones Gentry claims you shot a few hours ago. From behind the closed door of the kitchen."

"What about 'em?"

"You have the carcasses?"

I grin. "Not *on* me!"

Some of the men chuckle. But not many.

"Well, I ain't accusin' you of shootin' your prisoner," Ben says, "but I'd like to see them carcasses. Wouldn't the rest of you?"

Some would and some don't care. Rose says, "I was there when he shot them. It's true."

Ben removes his hat and says, "Well, pretty lady, I'd never call you a liar, but that seems awful convenient, since I never saw you before in my life, and think I'd remember you if I had."

"She's a close friend," I say.

Ben smiles. "All the more reason for suspicion. No offense, Ma'am."

"The rats are in the garbage bucket," Rose says. "I put them there myself."

"And did you dump the garbage bucket somewhere?"

"It's still in the kitchen, by the door, far as I know," she says.

"Well, if there's a bullet hole in each of 'em, I guess we can get back to drinkin' soon enough," Ben says. "Someone fetch the garbage bucket."

I look up at Rose. I know she had two rats, and know that Bose shot at them. But his gun misfired both times. If they produce two rats with no bullet holes, I'm gonna have some problems.

Rose's face gives nothin' away, so I'm lookin' around, to see if there's a way for me to make a break for it.

There's not. The whole room is crowded.

Wing Ding brings the garbage box into the center of the room, pokes around in it, and holds up two gunshot rats.

"Sorry to question, you, Sheriff," Ben says. "Please forgive me."

He hands me back the cloth badge, and I put it in my pocket and say, "I'm just sorry he managed to claw his way out of my jail hole. I think I need to build a wooden frame around it before we toss the next prisoner in there."

"I'll be glad to help you!" Ben says, and hoists a glass. "To the Sheriff!" he yells.

Everyone toasts me. While that's happenin', I look up at Rose, and notice she's got a serious look on her face. Before I can work my way to the steps, I hear a scream from the other side of the room, and see Constance sittin' on the floor, with seventeen-year-old Charlie Stallings's head in her lap. He looks unconscious.

"What happened?" I shout.

"He poked the bear!"

"Is he dead?"

"No, but he's unconscious."

"What happened?"

"Someone dared him."

I frown. Charlie Stallings must be a chuckle head. First, one-eyed Mary Burns kicks his ass. Now Rudy. I look out over the crowd and yell, "Who dared him?"

Everyone looks around. Finally three men at a card table feebly raise their hands.

"That's a three dollar fine," I say.

"There's no sign about a fine!" One of 'em says.

I frown. "Constance?"

"Yes sir?"

"Post a sign that says no one can dare anyone to make music or poke the bear."

"How much is the fine?"

"Ten dollars!"

The crowd gasps.

"I'm serious!" I yell. "Don't poke the bear! And don't dare anyone else to!"

Then I climb the stairs to see what's got Rose lookin' so serious.

CHAPTER 39

"LAWRENCE, KANSAS," ROSE says.

"What about it?"

"That's where it's going to happen."

"What is?" Gentry says.

"The massacre."

Gentry looks confused, so I tell her about the feelin' Rose had when she entered William Clarke's room.

"Who's that?"

"The school teacher who spent the night before Rose and Shrug came."

"What about him?"

"Rose thinks he's evil."

Rose says, "I had a bad feeling the minute I entered the room where Clarke spent the night. When I tried to sleep in the bed, I got hit with the worst visions I've had since I was a child."

"What kind of vision?" Gentry says.

"I saw people being dragged out of their homes, beaten and shot. Dozens and dozens. I saw their faces, from old men to little boys. They were begging and pleading for their lives. Their homes and businesses were set on fire. Hundreds of men attacked the town."

"Indians?" I say.

"No."

"Soldiers?"

"No."

"What type of men?"

"I don't know. But William Clarke was in charge."

I know I must appear mystified. "The *school* teacher?"

"He's not a school teacher, Emmett. At least, not in my vision."

"Clarke said he was gonna join the Missouri State Guard."

"The men in my vision don't appear to be soldiers," Rose says. "They could be, but that's not the feelling I get. They're not in uniform."

"Have your visions ever been wrong?" Gentry says.

"Yes. With regard to the timing. Sometimes I'm off by a year or more, because I see events, not dates. But the events I see always happen, eventually."

"If they always happen, there's nothing you can do to change them."

"Maybe. But I've never really tried to change them before. This time, I am."

I see her set her jaw. "What're you sayin', Rose?"

"I'm going to travel there and warn the town."

"You can't. They'll think you're either crazy, or..."

"Or a witch?" she says.

I nod.

"I'm willing to take the chance."

"I'll go with you," Gentry says.

"What?"

"Emmett, Rose can't go there alone. I want to help."

"They'll hang you both!"

"Then come with us."

"What about Rudy? What about sheriffin'? What about the saloon?"

"We'll just be gone a couple *weeks*," Emmett. "Wing can keep an eye out, and Constance can run the place for two weeks. As for sheriffin', you're allowed a couple weeks off."

I can't see what harm it'll do to try to warn people they could all be dead soon. "What would we tell the people of Lawrence?"

"We'll explain they'll be fine if they move away," Rose says.

I frown. "People don't like to leave their homes and businesses."

There's a knock at the door. "Emmett?"

It's Leah.

"Just a minute," I say.

"They'll leave their homes and businesses to keep from dying," Rose says.

"If we can convince 'em it's true," I say.

The knock at the door is repeated.

"Come on in, if it's so damned urgent!" I yell.

Leah bursts in, breathless.

"What?" I say.

"Billy the Kid is out front."

I roll my eyes.

"I'm serious. He's out there, and wants to kill you."

"He said that?"

"Yes! He yelled it for the whole saloon to hear. Said for someone to come get you or he'd start shootin' people in the street."

I shake my head. "It's always somethin'," I say.

CHAPTER 40

I WALK DOWNSTAIRS, out through the opening in the wall, and see a kid who can't be more than eighteen.

"Go on home, son," I say, but he's got his gun half out his holster before I can finish my speech.

I can see the kid is fast, and he started before I was ready, so I don't have time to pick my shot. I make my fastest draw, put two holes in his forehead, one in the center of his chest, while yellin', "I'm not payin' to bury him!" I turn and start walkin' back to the *Spur* before he finishes fallin' to the dirt.

"Oh my God!" Leah squeals. "You just killed Billy the Kid!"

"Oh, shut up," I said.

I wish I had a dollar for every Billy the Kid runnin' around the west, thinkin' he's some kind of outlaw. This is the third one I've shot in the past ten years, and I know of at least two others. Someday there'll probably be a *real* Billy the Kid gunslinger, and everyone'll think he's been around for twenty years.

Gentry meets me inside.

"I was so worried!" she says.

"Why?"

"What if he'd shot you?"

"Hell, Gentry, he weren't no more than a child. Don't know why these kids are so stupid. It really chaps me to kill 'em. He's probably got a Ma and Pa somewhere, and a brother I'll have to kill 'cause I killed this one. It's all so *stupid!*"

Them that were about to slap me on the back rightly decide I ain't in the mood, and they cut a wide path so I can walk upstairs to our bedroom to be alone. All I can think of is how a boy just threw his life away.

After a few minutes, Gentry and Rose come in and announce they want to leave tomorrow after breakfast to go warn the folks of Lawrence, Kansas. I can't imagine anyone packin' up and leavin' their homes and businesses because a couple of strangers show up tellin' tales of hundreds of men sackin' a town.

"You don't have to come, Emmett," Gentry says. "It's clear you're needed here. Shrug can escort us to Lawrence, and keep an eye on us."

"Shrug won't go in the town with you," I say.

"In the town, I'll have Rose to protect me."

"I still don't like it."

"We'll be okay," Rose says. "Gentry doesn't have to come, but I have to do this. I'll never sleep again if I don't make the effort."

I nod.

Then Gentry says, "But I *do* want to go, Emmett. Rose has always been there for you. She saved your life at least twice I know of, and probably again earlier today when Bose came up behind you. This is something I can do to help repay her."

I say, "Rose don't need repayin'. She's our friend."

"That's right, Gentry," Rose agrees.

"My mind's made up," Gentry says. "I want to go with her."

"Gentry, it's three hundred miles. And after Rose warns 'em, she'll be wantin' to continue on to Springfield, to be with Hannah."

The women look at each other. "I'd like to go," Gentry says, "but I don't want to burden you to have to bring me back."

I think on it a minute and say, "If you can wait two days, I'll get everything settled here, and I'll go with you. Rose, you can take the wagon, Gentry and I can ride horses, and when we've warned the folks of Lawrence, you can go on to Springfield, and I'll bring Gentry back.

Gentry's face lights up. "That'll be wonderful, Emmett. But we'll save time if Rose and I leave in the morning, and you can catch up with us."

To Rose, she says, "How far can we get each day driving oxen?"

"Thirty miles."

"And you can do how many on a horse, Emmett?"

"By myself? Sixty. More, if I push."

"So if we start tomorrow, and you come two or three days later, we'll be a third of the way there by the time you catch up to us."

Rose starts gettin' excited. "We'd stick to the main trail. You wouldn't be able to miss us."

"I'll wear a yellow bonnet," Gentry says. "Every day until you find us! And Shrug'll be nearby to take care of us."

"I know you'd enjoy spendin' time with Gentry," I say to Rose.

"I would, but I don't want to come between you," she says.

"Can I go with her Emmett?" Gentry says. "Please? It'd be *so* much fun! And then you'd be with us in three days or so!"

They've boxed me in a corner. If I say no, I'll break their hearts.

"Okay," I say. "But get all your female chat in early, because I just might meet up with you sooner than you think."

Gentry's smile tells me I made the right decision.

CHAPTER 41

THE NEXT TWO days are the loneliest I can remember. I work out my schedule with Mayor Ha-a-a-averford and the Town Council, then hire Mary Burns to help Constance oversee the saloon and workin' girls. Next, I work out a wage for Wing Ding to spend the nights at the *Spur* to make sure the whores are safe. I run all the errands and solve all the sheriffin' problems I can without actually leavin' town. The third mornin' after Rose and Gentry leave, I saddle Major, and the horse Bose Rennick left behind, a big gray horse I decide to name Steel. When I catch up to the women, Gentry's backside will be ready for a horse, after ridin' on a wagon bench all those miles.

I'm well-provisioned and so eager to start, I can't sleep. I leave a good three hours before daybreak and cover forty miles before stoppin' for the first time. I figure the woman have gone about seventy miles by now, which means if I push myself hard, I can catch 'em by this time tomorrow, at around the hundred-mile mark. I wouldn't stop at all today, but the horses ain't in shape for goin' all day without breaks, and I need to keep their well-bein' in mind.

I switch horses for two reasons. One, I want to make sure Steel is comfortable with me, and two, Major will benefit from not havin' to carry my weight all afternoon. The sun is shinin' bright and hot, and the trail is flat and dry. Steel is just as fine a horse as I thought he'd be, and I'm makin' excellent time. We're doin' so well I hate to pause long enough to eat, so I squeeze out another twenty miles before settlin' on a spot to water the horses. I figure they'll want a half hour of rest before we start movin' again.

There are hundreds of people travelin' the trail today, as always, and what was a very dangerous route just five years ago has become so well-populated by pioneers and settlers and travelers, you can scarcely go a mile without seein' fifty people at any given time. If Rose's wagon breaks down, someone would be along to fix it within minutes.

I usually travel my own trail, but don't want to take a chance on missin' the women in case somethin' happened to slow 'em down. The trail to Lawrence runs about four hundred yards wide for nearly three hundred miles. About every hour I see a wagon with oxen that looks like it could be Rose and Gentry, and even though I'm lookin' for a yellow bonnet on Gentry, I'm not gonna take a chance that she's removed it at the exact wrong time. So each time I slow down to check, I lose a few more minutes of precious time.

It's dusk now, and I've come further in one day than the women did in two, which means I'm about ten miles past where they made camp last night. If I'm right, that puts me about twenty miles behind 'em. I know Rose likes to head out at daybreak, so if I leave a couple hours before that, I could catch 'em as early as noon tomorrow. I wonder how often Gentry will look over her shoulder for me tomorrow, and hope it's a lot. I been cranin' my neck and concentratin' my eyes on so many people today I've given myself a huge headache.

The land out here is flat for a hundred miles, and in the dark I can see small fires burnin' all up and down the trail. I count more than fifty, some as close as a hundred feet away. The night is so quiet and still, I can hear the people from several campsites talkin' to each other. Most of these folks are friendly by need, but no one is goin' out of their way to approach me, which is the way I want it. I want to eat some beans, get some sleep, and hit the trail.

Next mornin' I get up, fry some bacon, soak my hard biscuits in a little water and push 'em around in the pan, and eat while drinkin' two cups of coffee. I get the horses ready, and start movin' along the trail. Then it dawns on me that I might be makin' a big mistake.

It's still dark. What if the women stopped for some reason? Rose's wagon could've needed a minor repair, or maybe she came across someone who needed doctorin'. Maybe they decided to travel with another family, for safety reasons, or because the other family requested help. If they made slower time for any reason, they could be within a few hundred yards of me right now, in which case, by leavin' in the dark, I might ride right past 'em and never run into 'em till they show up in Lawrence!

CHAPTER 42

IT'S DAYBREAK. I'VE sat for nearly two hours waitin' for this moment. My horses have to be wonderin' what the heck I've been doin', just sittin' in the dark between 'em, quiet with my thoughts of bein' with Gentry. Funny how you get used to a life with someone, and you just assume they'll be there when you wake up or go to sleep. Sometimes you have a picnic together and sometimes you bring your bear, and sometimes you're both too busy doin' other things to spend much time together, but you're both a shout away, so you're still together. Sometimes things are great and sometimes they ain't, but you know even durin' the bad times you can walk a few steps and make things better, or they can walk a few steps and do the same. Or you can both be pig-headed about some silly somethin' and keep your distance, but you're even doin' *that* together.

These last three days have taught me what it means to be apart from Gentry. We ain't actually been apart since we met, 'cept for a few days on our trip out west together, when I had to help carry Gentry's friend, Scarlett over the prairie by foot. 'Course, we weren't an official couple at that point, so it weren't as tough as these last three days.

I climb on Major and hold Steel on a lead, and before headin' east, I make a wide circle around the trail to make sure I haven't missed Gentry and Rose.

I haven't, so I start movin'.

Around one o'clock I'm passin' the trail that leads to Stafford, which tells me I'm a little more than a hundred miles east of Dodge. One of Emma's regulars hails from Stafford and swears it's exactly one hundred and five miles from Dodge. I don't know how he can be that accurate, but I know his calculation ain't far off at any rate.

Every moment of the ride I'm dartin' my head this way and that, concentratin' my focus on every wagon in sight, and that's about twenty a minute. But for the last two hours I know I'm close, very close, so I'm movin' slower and searchin' harder. There ain't no hills here, it's all flat. But there are some small rises that give you longer views. And it's right here, just beyond the trail that leads to Stafford, where I see somethin' a mile ahead that just sort of feels right. I stand in my stirrups, crane my neck, and focus on the wagon bein' pulled by two oxen, with what appears to be two women, and one of 'em wearin' what could be a yellow bonnet.

People are comin' and goin' in all directions. I see five Union soldiers headin' toward me at a trot. I wave at 'em, and they nod as they pass. I spur Major into a quick trot, not too fast just yet, 'cause I don't want to pass the *real* wagon while chasin' the one that *might* be carryin' my Gentry. It'd be easy to miss her and Rose, if they're travelin' wide, 'cause in this area the trail fans out more than a quarter mile. So I'm lookin' left and right, but concentratin' harder on the wagon in front of me, the one that's headin' up the next rise. I'm starin' as hard as I can, and suddenly I realize I don't have to stare so hard.

It's them!

Without a doubt, it's the two women I care most about in the world! Rose has the oxen exactly where they're supposed to be, right in the center of the trail, and they're just about to pass the next rise.

I'm ridin' as fast as I can now, without losin' Steel, and when I get a half mile behind the wagon, I shout, "Gentry!" at the top of my lungs.

She can't hear me yet. There's too much travelin' noise. The thirty or forty wagons in front and behind her are all makin' groanin', creaky, squeaky wagon sounds. And there's a wind blowin' left to right that's strong enough to drown my words.

But no matter. I'm ridin' swift, and I'll be on top of 'em in three minutes, on the other side of the rise. I wonder if Gentry will turn to see me barellin' in on 'em, just before they crest the small hill. It'd be the perfect place to turn around and look.

But I hope she don't turn around and see me, 'cause I got a fun idea.

I'm gonna crest the hill and slow down, and just sort of sneak up on 'em with a speed walk. I'm gonna slide right past 'em, like I've never seen 'em before in my life, and as I pass, I'll turn toward 'em and tip my hat and say, "Ladies," and keep goin' twenty or thirty yards before turnin' around and grinnin'.

Rose'll roll her eyes and smile, but Gentry'll think it's hilarious.

They're crestin'. *Don't turn around, Gentry, you'll spoil the surprise!*

They hit the crest, Gentry turns halfway around to the right, bless her heart, but I'm comin' up behind 'em on the left, and just before she can pivot and look the other way, their wagon is headin' down the other side of the slope. I'm two minutes behind, and I can't wait. I spur Major into a canter and silently swear I'm never gonna leave Gentry's side again, as long as I live. My horse is flyin', my heart's racin', but everything goes black a minute, and when I come to, I find I'm lyin' on the ground, on my back. And my head feels like someone smacked me with a two by four. And when the five Union soldiers gather around me, I feel like things may have taken a bad turn.

"*Gentry*!" I scream with all my might.

At least I think I screamed her name before I blacked out again.

CHAPTER 43

FORT BEND IS north of Stafford, west of Wichita, and fifteen miles from where I was shot in the back of the head. I'm on a cot in the infirmary, and horrified to hear about the wound in my head.

Horrified because I was barely hit.

How could a glancin' blow knock me off my horse and make me black out five or ten times durin' the journey to the fort? All I can figure is, it caught me by surprise and I must've landed on my head when I hit the ground.

While I might a' hit my head, my entire body's achin', so I obviously took quite a tumble. I remember goin' at a fast clip when I was struck. I'm surly and furious over getting' that close to Gentry, only to be taken a good thirty miles outta my way.

Why the hell did someone shoot me, and why did they feel compelled to bring me here to patch me up afterward?

It don't make sense.

It's mornin', so I've had a good night's sleep. Now I need to take a piss. Despite the aches and pains, I feel strong. I sit up in my cot, feel the bandaged tender spot on the side of my head, and know I'm good enough to travel. I could cut a straight path from here to Daindridge, and save a full day of ridin', but can't take the chance of missin' the wagon by getting' in front of 'em. If that happened, I wouldn't see Gentry till Lawrence, six days from now. If I don't catch up to Gentry before then, she'll be worried sick about me. She's probably already upset, havin' figured to meet up with me sometime yesterday.

I'll backtrack to the place I got shot, then follow the trail I know Rose is takin'. I'll ride my horses into the ground if I have to. By this time tomorrow, I'll be in Gentry's arms, even if I have to carry the horses!

I climb out of my cot, find a piss jar, and use it. Then I look around for my clothes.

"You seen my clothes?" I say to the guy I just noticed lyin' in a cot next to mine.

He don't answer, just shakes his head. Now that I get a good look, I can see the poor kid's in a bad way. He's lost an arm. His face is pale and his teeth are chatterin'. I'm no doctor, but I've seen enough injuries to know this kid is on the fence.

"What's your name, son?" I whisper, so as not to disturb the other three patients I now see in the room.

He tries to speak, but nothin' comes out. I reach out and pat his shoulder.

"You'll be okay," I say. "You're gonna make it."

His eyes search mine to see if I'm bein' truthful. I nod and say, "I'm positive."

His hand moves out from under the blanket. I take it and say, "Stay strong."

He squeezes my hand. A tear falls from his eye. I nod again, put his hand back under the blanket, take the blanket from my cot, and cover him with it. As I'm doin' that, tuckin' the blanket around his feet, I realize he's lost a leg, as well.

I walk around the room, lookin' for my clothes. They're not here, so I open the door and start walkin' down the hall.

"Looks like you're doin' better," a soldier says, comin' up behind me.

"You the doctor?"

"I am."

"Thanks for patchin' me up."

"Much obliged."

"That kid in there."

"Which one?"

"The one lyin' next to me, no arm and leg. Will he make it?"

"I'm bettin' no. But God might feel different about it."

"I'll pray for him."

"Can't hurt."

We stand there a few moments, thinkin' about the kid, me in my under clothes, him in his uniform.

"I'll be needin' my clothes and belongin's," I say.

"Come with me," he says.

CHAPTER 44

THE DOC LEADS me outside to the courtyard, where I see a dozen soldiers doin' one thing or another, and three men dressed in gray uniforms.

"Go over there and stand with them," he says. "The Colonel will be out directly."

As he starts to leave, I put my hand on his arm.

"Who're those three?"

"Johnny Rebs."

"What's that mean?"

He looks at me like I've lost my mind. "We're at war. They're rebels."

"The southern states have uniforms already?" I say.

"They do. This war's been planned a long time."

"I'm Emmett Love, Sheriff of Dodge City."

He seems a nice man. But when I tell him who I am, he says somethin' that gives me pause. What he says is, "Glad to meet you, Sheriff. I'm the Queen of England."

As I watch him walk off, I hear someone shout, "You there! Get your ass over here."

I turn to see who he's talkin' to, and it appears to be me. I walk over to him, and he tells me to stand in line with the others. He's got a gun, and several others with guns are watchin' us, so I figure the line is where I ought to be until I can straighten things out with the Colonel.

As it turns out, me and the three Johnny Rebs are in line a full hour, which puts Gentry and Rose that much further away. I'm tryin' to hold my temper because, honestly, I'm caught up in the middle of a war. As Sheriff of Dodge City, I'm exempt from soldierin', and the good news for me is, Kansas went with the Northern side, and I'm Sheriff of a Kansas town. If I'd been shot and taken to a southern fort, they might not turn me loose!

Finally, the Colonel and a Sergeant show up. The Sergeant makes us stand in a straight line. I expect them to ask us a few questions, but they ask us nothin'. Instead, the Colonel clears his throat and starts makin' a speech.

"As you men know, we're at war. Unlike wars of the past, this one pits brother against brother, father against son, and neighbor against neighbor. It's a helluva thing. And Kansas is wrapped up in it completely against our will. I don't like this war. But I'll do my duty, as I'm sworn to. What really chaps my ass is the whole damned thing could've been avoided."

He shakes his head and continues: "My people come from Tennessee. They just want to be left alone to live their lives and raise their families. Now I hear the war is headin' their way, and people I grew up with are going to die for reasons they don't even understand."

He shakes his head again. "Ain't this a helluva war?"

It is. And I'm not sure the Colonel actually said why he thinks the war was avoidable. But he's right about how almost no one really knows why they're fightin'. I mean, they're probably all told somethin' by their commanders that gets their dander up, but that don't make it accurate. Or maybe it *is* accurate, I don't know. But if *I* don't know, then *they* probably don't, either. What I *do* know, it ain't *my* war, and I wouldn't participate if it was. These are Americans fightin' Americans and I'd take my own life before shootin' my relatives over the color of their uniform, or over issues I don't understand. Mostly, I think those who kill each other in this war will be shootin' not because of some political cause, but because they don't want to get shot.

The Colonel continues: "This war is different in other ways. It's the first industrial war. Railroads, telegraphs, ships, steamboats, and mass-produced weapons will all play a part. And that's where you men come in. You're prisoners of war. As such, you'll work from sunup to sundown to help us get a railroad built. It's in your best interest, because the railroad will bring troops and supplies up and down the war front six times faster than troops can move on foot. There are no finer generals than the south has, and no finer troops, although we like to feel we do a damn fine job with our troops, as well. I mean, we were all on the same side a few months ago. But the railroads and factories will win this fight for the North, and the faster we build this railroad, the faster you men can get home to your loved ones."

"You'll be leaving here in an hour, and transported to the job site. It's a rotten position you're in, and I feel for you, and that's the truth. But if you keep your mouth shut and your muscles working, you'll come through this alive. You have my word."

He starts to leave, and a couple of soldiers come up behind us.

"Colonel?" I say.

He turns to look at me. "Did I just tell you to keep your mouth shut?"

"I ain't a *soldier*!" I say. "I'm—"

...I'm in a wagon on my back, movin' across the prairie. The three Johnny Rebs are starin' vacantly at the scenery. My head is foggy and I feel somethin' heavy on my feet. I think one of the prisoners might be sittin' on my ankles, so I sit up to complain about it, and realize I'm wearin' leg irons.

CHAPTER 45

THE PRISONERS DON'T talk much, but one whispers I got conked on the head with a rifle butt.

"Why?" I whisper back. "I'm not a soldier."

"They claimed you're a horse thief. Said you were leadin' one of the Colonel's stolen horses."

"I'm the sheriff of Dodge," I whisper. "I had a badge in my pocket."

"Maybe you killed the sheriff and took his badge."

"Shut up you two!" one of the guards shouts at us.

When we get where we're goin', there are maybe twenty prisoners, and eight guards with rifles. There's a hand cart on a track, and an actual train car about fifty yards away. As I learn over the next few hours, every 160 feet of track that gets laid, the prisoners have to push and pull the rail car back and forth over the new section to see if it works. According to the other prisoners, it takes two days for sixteen prisoners to lay 160 feet of track and test the car. Of course, every day more prisoners and guards will be brought in, which will speed the work up considerably.

For me, the next few days are all about acclimatin'.

I'm on the sledge hammer crew.

The hand cart brings me and five other men a pile of rocks. We crush 'em, and a prisoner named Eddie scoops and hauls the rock chips away in a wheelbarrow. The rocks are placed on the ground to make a path, and wooden crossties are placed on our broken rocks. Then, two lengths of iron rails are laid on top of the crossties four feet apart, and a well-trained sledge hammer man drives iron spikes into the wood on each side of the rail. The spikes have a lip on one side that holds the rail in place. The rails are sixteen feet long, and weigh 120 pounds each.

I rise at dawn, work all day, get fed a meager amount twice a day, sleep in a tent at night that's guarded by soldiers. There's little talk among the prisoners, and less involvin' me, since I'm widely considered a horse thief. The guards are harsh, but not abusive. When one soldier breaks out into song, and is punished, I think about Rudy, and wonder how he's doin'.

Of course I think about Gentry.

I think about Rose, and Shrug, and *The Lucky Spur*, and the town of Dodge, and how wonderful our lives had been only recently. But mostly I think of Gentry. I think of her night and day. She's the first thought I have in the mornin', and the last thought I have at night.

I don't dream often.

I think that's because I'm in constant pain from the leg shackles and exhausted by the non-stop work. I laugh to myself, thinkin' how hard I thought it was to build a jail hole. That *was* hard work, but at least Wing and I switched jobs every other day. This sledge hammer work jars your bones with every hit, and wears your back out somethin' fierce, and I don't have any of Rose's liniment to put on it at night.

But when I *do* dream, it's always about Gentry. Makin' sweet love to her. Hearin' her voice askin' if we can lay under the blanket just a little longer. Hearin' the waterfall of laughter that spills outta her mouth when Rudy chases and knocks the crap outta me while playin' tag. Sometimes I dream about the trip we took from Rolla to Dodge last year. Think about the times we lay together under the stars. Think about the fireflies at Firefly Heaven in East Kansas. The great White River Nipple Contest, where somehow she got bested by skinny little Leah.

I smile, just thinkin' about the dreams. Wish I'd come up with a way to memorize those special moments while I was havin' 'em, so I could remember every part of 'em. Like how her hair smells comin' in from a rain. Or what sounds I was hearin' that day when Gentry went dashin' off and threw herself into a mud puddle full speed and slid nearly twenty feet. The whores travelin' with us joined in, and before long they were laughin' and rollin' around in the mud, and slappin' pads of it in each other's hair. Then Gentry said, "What about you, Emmett?" and before I knew it, the whores dragged me into the puddle, pushed and poked and rolled me around, and slapped my face with mud cakes, and laughed and giggled. But when it suddenly grew quiet, I noticed it was Gentry layin' on top of me, kissin' my cheeks and mouth.

At that moment, all the others backed away, silently, realizin' somethin' special was happenin'.

"I like you, Emmett," Gentry had said to me that day.

God, I miss that girl.

CHAPTER 46

I'VE LOST TRACK of days.

One blends into the next, when you get no news, and aren't allowed to talk. It's endless day after endless day, and your beard starts to grow and your clothes wear out. I'd been in my unders all this time, but when one of the workers dies they put me in his rebel uniform. I feel bad for the boy that died, but I'm warmer at night, when it's cold.

I wonder what Gentry thought when I didn't show up. I know they would a' gone on to Lawrence to warn the people about the massacre. But Gentry would a' been beside herself with worry. Rose would a' said I probably passed them in the night, and would be waitin' for 'em in Lawrence.

But I weren't in Lawrence when they got there.

After warnin' the folks, did Gentry go on to Springfield with Rose, thinkin' I'd come there to find her? Rose would want to do that, since her adopted daughter, Hannah, was there. Or did Rose or Shrug bring her all the way back to Dodge? Knowin' Rose, my best guess is, she took Gentry to Springfield, which is only a few days away, and probably sent Shrug back to Dodge to check on me. Shrug can cover fifty miles a day on foot. He could make the trip from Lawrence to Dodge and back to Springfield in sixteen days.

I'm tryin' to do the cipher in my head, but I'm out of practice and have to give up several times.

It's another day, and I hoist the hammer, bring it down on what feels like the millionth rock, feel the shudder go through my bones, and frown, realizing this particular rock hasn't broken. I wonder where all these rocks come from? Who brings 'em to the hand cart people? I lift the hammer up over my head and bring it down a second time, with all my strength. This here's an ornery rock. Two blows and it hasn't busted. That's a rare thing, in my experience. I hoist again, and this time it breaks into five pieces. On the one hand, I'm sad, because I like to think of my spirit as bein' like this tough rock, able to withstand anythin'. On the other hand, it gives me a strange feelin' of satisfaction. Maybe that's because it's the only way to tell I'm alive. If I keep poundin' on a rock that don't break, maybe I'm dead and haven't realized it yet.

I stop a minute and look at the five pieces of stone, and smile, rememberin' that every time Shrug and I traveled durin' our two years together, he'd be up ahead, scoutin' the territory. Occasionally he'd set four stones on the ground, representin' north, south, east, and west. A fifth stone would show the direction I was supposed to follow.

The one thing I think about with every swing of the hammer is bustin the chain off my ankles. The daily rubbin' against my bare skin creates wounds that, like the rope in Rudy's nose, never heal. They open up every mornin', and hurt all day. I get rock dust in 'em constantly, and they get infected and ooze pus and blood all the time. And the skin around 'em is always blistered and chapped. The soldiers give me salve to put on 'em regular, and that helps keep the infection down, but it don't stop the pain. I don't suffer like Rudy done, but I understand his sufferin' more than I used to. I hate that I danced with him that first night when I didn't know any better, but proud I shot the piano, and the spurs off Hollis Williams' boots.

I smile, thinkin' about how Gentry loved to tease me about Rudy bein' my son.

I pound the pieces into smaller ones and try to remember what I was thinkin'. Oh yeah, the cipherin' of Gentry's trip. So figure seven days for Rose to get to Lawrence, two more days to realize I ain't there, six days for Shrug to walk all the way back to Dodge to check on me, another to realize I ain't there either, and eight more to walk the 400 miles from Dodge to Springfield.

I don't know how long I've been here, bustin' rocks, but it's probably been long enough for Shrug to have made his round trip. I think of poor Gentry, and what must be goin' through her mind. Will she stay in Springfield with Rose or go back to Dodge? She don't know it, but she's got a legal claim to *the Spur*. I put it in both our names. Someone will eventually tell her that, and I can only hope it's me.

Each day we're movin' further west. There's more than fifty of us now, and nearly thirty guards. I have no idea how far west we've come since I was forced into railroad labor, but it's significant, as we're now doin' more than 300 feet a day. The days keep meltin' one after the other, and the only thing that changes is the scenery.

Until one swelterin' August afternoon, when all hell breaks loose.

CHAPTER 47

I HAD JUST busted the last piece from a giant rock and signaled Eddie to come shovel the pieces into his wheel barrow. It ain't my job to help him do that, and I'd get punished if I tried to, since that eight minutes or so between loads is the only time I get to put my hammer down and sit. I'm sittin' there, lookin' at the size of the rocks they're getting' ready to bring me later this afternoon and can't imagine tryin' to bust 'em, they're so big. As always, my thoughts turn to Gentry, and I try to imagine her lyin' next to me, and hope she ain't forgotten or given up on me yet. I'm much older than she is, and it would make sense for her to move on and find a young feller to raise a family with.

I hope she don't, but she probably should.

Those are the thoughts I'm havin' this hot afternoon in August when the first shots are fired. Everyone ducks for cover, as a band of men come ridin' their horses hell bent for leather from the east.

The guards have never been fired on since I been here, and they're in a panic. Several go down from that first wave. But the rest take up positions behind whatever structures they can, and begin returnin' fire, which makes the attackers turn tail and gallop off.

Just as the guards begin celebratin', another band of men attacks 'em from the west! They don't appear to be shootin' at anyone wearin' gray, but the blue coats are fallin' like flies. Just as the guards turn to face the new enemy, another group comes at 'em from the east again, and gets 'em in a crossfire. It quickly becomes clear that the attackers are just playin' with the guards, because they keep dartin' in and out from either side, back and forth, usin' a push me-pull you kind of strategy.

Within minutes, the outdoor guards are out of ammunition. They stand to surrender, and are cut down by enemy fire. The only guards with ammunition are the five or six who were in the railroad car when the attack started. But they don't last long. Every time one of 'em tries to take a shot, a hundred attackers shoot back. There must be three, maybe four hundred men doin' the attackin'. When the battle's over, twenty or thirty of 'em bust through the railroad car door and remove all the ammunition and weapons and then gather the guns from the dead guards on the ground.

When the prisoners realize the battle's over and the guards dead, they stand up and cheer fit to beat the band.

I cheer right along with 'em.

We all move to the area where the horsemen have congregated. They accept our cheers and accolades for a minute, and then motion us to quiet down.

A lone rider comes up from somewhere behind them, and works his way through the center of the sea of horses and riders. When he speaks, I recognize his voice.

It's William Clarke, the school teacher.

CHAPTER 48

"YOU MEN ARE free," Clarke says. "Go back to your homes, rest up, get provisioned, and rejoin the fight. I only wish I could spend more time with you, help you get those chains and shackles off, give you weapons and supplies for your journey. But we've got pressing business that can't wait, and the war hangs in the balance. The South has recently suffered a heavy loss on the battle field, and we aim to make up for it. If we're to win this war, we'll require your valiant efforts. Can we count on you?"

The roar from our fifty men is thunderous.

Clarke continues. "That's mighty gratifying. Mighty gratifying, indeed. But we need you at full strength, so go back to your homes, check on the welfare of your family members, and then come back and fight with a vengeance!"

Every man cheers, except me. I have no intention of fightin' anybody. When the cheers die down, I call out, "Mr. Clarke?"

He rides closer to me.

"Do I know you, sir?"

"I'm Emmett Love. Sheriff, Dodge City."

He gives me a long look. "I don't think so."

"It's true. Under all these whiskers, I'm he."

He says, "If you are, then what's the sign say around the neck of that bear?"

I smile at the thought. "Don't Poke the Bear!"

He smiles back. "Well, in that case, I suppose I've repaid your kindness. How goes it with you, sir?"

I look around, gesture to the rock pile, to the dead guards, to the prisoners who mostly look worse than me. "How the fuck do you think?"

Everyone looks around, wonderin' what's gonna happen next. But Clarke begins chucklin' a moment, and then he laughs. Then the men around him laugh, and the men around me laugh. Even I start to laugh.

"Can I ask you what day it is?" I say.

"It's Wednesday. Why, you got a train to catch?"

The men around him roar with laughter.

"What's the date?" I say. "It's August, right?"

"It *is* August," he says. "August 19th, 1863."

I fall to the ground.

"Are you okay, Sheriff?"

I shake my head. I couldn't have heard him right.

"Excuse me. Did you say 1863?"

"Yes, of course. What year did you think it was?"

"1861."

He shakes his head. "You poor bastards."

And with that, he and his men ride away.

CHAPTER 49

I KNOW IT won't be long before Union soldiers are all over the place. The Rebel soldiers are bandin' together, lookin' for any guns and ammunition the attackers left behind, and strippin' the bodies of any money the soldiers might have on 'em.

"Look for keys!" I shout. "Maybe we can get these chains off!"

It strikes me as odd no one else thought about that yet, but after twenty minutes of searchin', we come to the conclusion that whoever put these chains on us had no intention of removin' 'em, since there's not a single key to be found.

I trudge back to my rock pile, lay the chain atop a stout rock, and lay into it, and get nothin' for my effort except a shootin' pain in my wrists and forearms from the recoil.

I hit it again and again, to no avail. Some of the other men are trying to break their chains with sledge hammers, but most have given up and moved out. One by one they quit, figurin' to get as far away from this spot as possible. They can always deal with the chains later.

Personally, I want to give it one more try. I reposition the chain against a sharp rock, put all my strength into it, every last ounce I have, and...

...and my sledge hammer breaks when I hit the chain.

I shriek a curse to the sky, then look down and notice the chain in two pieces.

When the last Rebel soldier has gone, I drag both ends of chain behind me and strip the pants off a dead Union soldier, and take them with me, along with some twine and a piece of sharp metal I kick off the side of the supply door that was left hangin' after Clarke's attackers busted in. When I get far from all the Rebel soldiers, I'll put the Union pants on, and keep to the tall grass, so if anyone sees me, they'll just see my white undershirt.

I'm goin' to Dodge.

I have no idea how far away I am, and don't care. I only know I'm gonna walk day and night till I get there, because even if Gentry ain't in Dodge, at least I know the locals, and can get the blacksmith to cut these damn leg irons off me once and for all.

I don't know if Gentry'll be in Dodge, but that's my first guess. I haven't seen her for two years and four months, but someone will have told her long ago that she owns half of the *Spur*. Even if she believes I'm dead, it was our dream

CHAPTER 50

AFTER SIX HOURS of headin' southwest, I make my way to the top of a short rise and see in the distance hundreds of horses and riders headin' east and west, which tells me I'm about two miles from the main trail. I also have a general idea of where I am, and I'm quite pleased about it. I don't want to walk anywhere near the main trail because I'm wearing Union pants, and someone might take me for a deserter.

The good news is I no longer have to drag my chains behind me. I've tied them to my lower legs with the twine I found in the railroad car. It's terribly uncomfortable trying to walk this way, but I can cover more ground at a faster pace. I've also got two pieces of beef jerky I found in a can in the railroad car that no one took, so that ought to do me till I get back home.

Which ain't all that far.

Over the past two years we've apparently laid around sixty miles of track, which puts me about forty miles northeast of Dodge.

I stay low and keep walkin'. I look all around, same way I did two years ago when I was travelin' the main road, lookin' for Gentry and Rose. Only this time I don't want to see anyone. While Union soldiers might shoot me for desertin', Rebel soldiers will shoot me for wearin' these pants. I'm also on the edge of where Indians used to be a few years back, and you never know if a few might've returned to hide. There's game here, and woods less than a mile north, so it's possible I could run into some hostiles.

For these reasons, and others,' every time I think I hear somethin', I jump down into the tall grass and lie there on my belly a half hour, till I'm completely convinced there's nothin' around me.

The more I think about it, the more I think I should get closer to the woods. The chances of runnin' into Indians is smaller than runnin' into soldiers, 'cause I'm traveling near Fort Dodge. If I *do* see soldiers, I can dart into the woods and hide.

I'll lose thirty minutes of time, headin' back to the wood line, but I figure it's a smart gamble. As I head northwest, I see the sun goin' down. I'm not gonna stop till I get to Dodge, but thirty miles, walkin' with chains on my legs, is a hard walk in the tall grass.

Based on the position of the moon, I'm guessin' it's after four in the mornin'. I'm travelin' at a clip of two miles per hour, by a sliver of moonlight that's barely sufficient to keep me just south of the tree line that runs all the way to the Arkansas River. This is a good route to take, because it's north of Fort Dodge.

Now I'm about ten miles northeast of Dodge City, barely able to contain my enthusiasm, knowin' each step I take is bringin' me that much closer to Gentry's arms.

In the same instant that I'm the most elated I've been in more than two years, I hear something movin' in the woods less than a hundred yards away.

I stop and drop. But the sound don't stop.

It's gettin' louder.

Whoever it is, they've seen me. They know I'm here. They're gettin' closer.

I jump to my feet and start runnin' fast as I can, through the tall grass. But I'm wearin' leg irons and chains, and feel like I'm movin' slow as molasses.

They're gainin' on me.

The tall grass is whippin' my arms, neck and face, and I only get about ten yards before they shoot me in the back.

And just as I did the last time this happened, two years and four months ago, I scream, "*Gentry!*"

CHAPTER 51

I'M LYIN' HERE in the grass. My shoulder don't hurt half as much as I expected, but there's a reason for that, and the reason is, I didn't get shot in the first place.

I'm lyin' here, waitin' to see what might happen next, and realize I never heard a gunshot, and I ain't bleedin'.

So I weren't shot, which is a good thing.

On the other hand, somethin' hit me hard enough to knock me down, so that's a bad thing. I'm not unconscious this time, and there's no Union soldiers standin' around me, so right now the good things outweigh the bad.

Except that I see and hear nothin'. It's an eerie quiet, like bein' in the center of a storm, when your hair starts to rise before the bad part hits.

I wonder if maybe some Indians started to attack me and changed their minds. Maybe one of 'em hit me with a tomahawk.

I lie here quiet as possible till my breathin' gets back to normal. Whoever's out there seems to have given me a pass.

I look up at the stars and mouth a silent thank you.

Then I get to my feet and start walkin'.

Within seconds, I get knocked down again.

And then I hear the craziest sound.

It's like the bleat of a goat.

But it ain't a goat, it's a bear.

A bear that's playin' tag, and laughin' at me.

At first, I'm the happiest man on earth.

But then I realize somethin' awful must a' happened, if Rudy's been turned loose.

I hug my bear and try not to think about what might've happened. I'll know soon enough when I get to Dodge in a few hours.

Right now, I just want to hug my bear.

In a few minutes, I'll start walkin' again. But right now I'm huggin' Rudy, and he's huggin' me, and laughin' his silly head off.

It don't take long for me to realize I ain't so much huggin' Rudy as I'm huggin' Gentry, Rose, Shrug, and everythin' I've lost, and everythin' I hope to get back.

Wherever Gentry is, I'll find her. Whatever's happened, I'll deal with it.

I won't lie. I'm worried.

But this silly, laughin' bear deserves a game of tag, and though my heart ain't in it, I aim to give him one before I head for Dodge. I rush into the darkness where I know he's waitin', and tag him, and he knocks me on my ass.

EPILOGUE

AT 7:00 A.M. ON Friday, August 21, 1863, two days after killing twenty-eight guards and freeing Dodge City Sheriff Emmett Love and fifty-two Confederate prisoners, William Clarke Quantrill descended upon the town of Lawrence, Kansas, with a force of 450 men. Quantrill's Raiders looted every person, home and business, and robbed the town's bank. Under Quantrill's orders, 183 men and boys were dragged from their homes and executed in front of their horrified mothers, wives, and sisters. By 9:00 a.m., it was over. Every male in Lawrence above the age of thirteen lay dead, and every structure in town had been set on fire.

THE END

Special Offer from John Locke!

If you like my books, you'll LOVE my mailing list! By joining, you'll receive discounts of up to 67% on future eBooks. Plus, you'll be eligible for amazing contests, drawings, and you'll receive immediate notice when my newest books become available!

Visit my website:
http://www.DonovanCreed.com

John Locke

New York Times Best Selling Author
8th Member of the Kindle Million Sales Club
(which includes James Patterson, Stieg Larsson,
George R.R. Martin and Lee Child, among others)

John Locke had 4 of the top 10 eBooks on
Amazon/Kindle at the same time, including #1 and #2!

...Had 6 of the top 20, and 8 books in the
top 43 at the same time!

...Has written 19 books in three years in
four separate genres, all best-sellers!

...Has been published in numerous languages by many of the
world's most prestigious publishing houses!

Donovan Creed Series:

Lethal People

Lethal Experiment

Saving Rachel

Now & Then

Wish List

A Girl Like You

Vegas Moon

The Love You Crave

Maybe

Callie's Last Dance

Emmett Love Series:

Follow the Stone

Don't Poke the Bear

Emmett & Gentry

Goodbye, Enorma

Dani Ripper Series:

Call Me

Promise You Won't Tell?

Dr. Gideon Box Series:

Bad Doctor

Box

Other:

Kill Jill

Non-Fiction:

How I Sold 1 Million eBooks in 5 Months!

Made in the USA
Lexington, KY
10 June 2016